Has innovated quite a bit in the realm of
modern odia short stories.
- **Dr. Sitakanta Mohapatra**
Eminent Poet, Critic

There is originality in Rajanikanta's thoughts.
His philosophical realisation is sharp.
- **Manoj Das**
Eminent Story Teller, Essayist

I am overwhelmed by the intrinsic dynamism
of Rajanikanta's language and theme.
- **Chittaranjan Das**
Eminent Scholar, Philosopher, Critic.

The Golden Jackal
& Other Stories

Rajanikanta Mohanty

Translation by
Brajamohan Mishra

 BLACK EAGLE BOOKS
2022

 BLACK EAGLE BOOKS

USA address:
7464 Wisdom Lane
Dublin, OH 43016

India address:
E/312, Trident Galaxy, Kalinga Nagar,
Bhubaneswar-751003, Odisha, India

E-mail: info@blackeaglebooks.org
Website: www.blackeaglebooks.org

First International Edition Published by
BLACK EAGLE BOOKS, 2022

THE GOLDEN JACKAL & OTHER STORIES
by **Rajanikanta Mohanty**

Translation by **Brajamohan Mishra**

Original Copyright © Sakuntala Mohanty
Translation Copyright © Brajamohan Mishra

Cover & Interior Design: Ezy's Publication

ISBN- 978-1-64560-246-0 (Paperback)
Library of Congress Control Number: 2022931033

Printed in United States of America

Disclaimer
This is a work of fiction.All characters, organizations and situations are of author's imagination and any resemblance to any person, organization or situation is purely co-incidental." The author respects all individuals, organisations and communities and there is no intention in these stories to hurt any individual, organisation or community.

IN MEMORIUM of
my poet mother Swarnalata Mohanty
my teacher father Biswanath Mohanty

- Rajanikanta

Translator's Note

Like a face in the crowd, Rajanikanta Mohanty stands obviously apart from the host of golden daffodils of Odia story tellers. Because his apprehension of the multifoliate reality cascading rhythmically all around is, by all means, novel but natty. His sensitive response as a superb creative genius to the panorama and pageantry of contemporary human frailties and frivolities commands both respect and love of enlightened readers. His universe, by no means, registers any hanky-panky since his absolute and obsessive fidelity to experience is unobtrusive and intuitive. In him the reader meets a genius that speaking to men, enters and possesses him/her emotionally and intellectually. A seasoned timber, Rajanikanta has already carved a niche for himself in heterogeneous readers' hearts. In fact, one does not find very many Odia story tellers like him. The stories I have translated and which form this volume exemplify his satisfying and salubrious departure (In fact Rajani's trademark) from the hackneyed way of pitching' the yarn especially thematically. In this connection, it won't be wide off the mark to remark that he is a literary seer who sees and shows the 'Viswarupa' (cosmic form) of our existence.

Brajamohan Mishra

CONTENTS

ANTS

A dry leaf fell on the ground touching Swetanka's body. Swetanka was neither startled nor frightened .But it's wrong to hold that it did not float a white boat along the blue lake of his mind. The silent moon above the entire town, a meadow along the horizon got flooded. Beams freckled through the banyan tree leaves. Strange, wild wind travels, leaves getting dried and falling ! Is it possible? Swetanka remained sitting under that tree on a meadow half furlong away from the town. Eight o'clock, a very moon-blanched night. After taking meal in a hotel he used to come to this tree paddling his bicycle and return to his residence at ten o'clock. Even though he was regular in the habit, he had never witnessed a dry leaf falling in night producing such sound. Why does a dry leaf produce sound when it falls from a tree? Born silently, it dies in sound! What about man? Born in sound, dies silently, alone, apprising none. A bit dejected, he gathered the leaf and put it in his pocket. A dry leaf falling in a serene moon-bathed night; isn't it an accomplishment?

Night turning moonlit, a dry leaf falling from a tree in such a night, Swetanka squatting under a banyan tree every night and keeping the fallen dry leaf in a pocket considering it to be an achievement, thinks it impossible on his part to complete a story with these ingredients.

Because he is not in favour of shortening a story contracting life with finitude. That's why, editors of magazines do not publish his stories with a caution that his stories must be comparatively short. But Swetanka remains impervious and thinks, " Let my stories remain unpublished and life be unexpressed, but it is impossible on my part to write comparatively short stories and lead a contracted life. Where life gets confined words become immobile."

Of course, he feels tormented with the pain of remaining unexpressed. He can't plant a kiss on Sudipa's cheek even when he gets her in a lonely dark room. He turns apprehensive that Sudipa might not be prepared for that. He considers all dramatic happenings to be assaults. That's why he is so much unexpressed. On the contrary, he glares at twenty or twenty five labourers, male and female, working together at a little distance and residing in a single shed. Couples make love and act too. They are busy, they are active, they are lively, their words are attractive, so liquid and mobile!

Here also Swetanka's story is not finished. Because it won't end, it's getting late to begin. Since he is unable to decide where from and how he should begin his life sketch, he is swayed by others' stories and he becomes disconnected. So, listening to others, studying other minds, reading others' stories, he lives.

STORY 1

Swetanka! Why are you so indifferent towards your family? What has happened to you? Since you are the eldest son, you must think that you have to shoulder more responsibilities. But I apprehend our family will be ruined because of your indolence. Why are you so complacent? You are already employed for four years. But you send home a paltry amount this month and no amount that. Yet I have not grudged or grumbled a little. Even I have not yet written to you about this. But things are getting beyond control. I shall retire after a year. What will be the fate of this family? You have seven younger brothers and sisters. How will they grow? Won't you shoulder the responsibilities of the family? Rohit says, brother is living comfortably because of his service and he never thinks of our condition. He simply writes down something after getting relieved from office and sends it to magazines at his own expense. He spends a lot for them those who are idle, book worms, and writes day in and day out. So, how can he get time to think of us? We have no relationship with him anymore. I don't feel I have an elder brother.

Swetanka! In the last three years we have not been able to give Sanju in marriage. You haven't yet let me know how much you could contribute towards her marriage. Sanju herself expressed that she won't marry. Now she is attached to one Prajapita Brahma Kumari Ashram which she visits daily. I can't prohibit her. In fact, how can I? She is past twenty-eight, yet unmarried. Yes, your mother cautioned her more than once but she replied that divine life is more peaceful than this mundane one. Your mother fell ill and was hospitalized. I know how much pain and suffering I have undergone on that account. Now she is as frail as a banana leaf. Send some money this month. This is March, I know the field staff get some amount of money towards their T.A, Medicine bill, etc. They give some percentage of it to the clerks concerned. I think you will get some amount towards that. Take my words into your heart otherwise all will blame you later on as you are the eldest son. Writing is of no avail, all meaningless. How does it benefit anybody ? Only your name will figure in history.

Writing means you are ruining your health, burning midnight oil and wasting money.

From this story Swetanka derived a storyline of his village mate Sarat's letter- 'You might not have known that auntie had to undergo abortion of her ninth child by quackery. She became fatally ill and was hospitalized. Our distressed uncle had to undergo vasectomy as a father of only two children requesting a lot to the doctor. Do you know why? The money he got from the operation as per the provision of the family planning programme was spent on auntie's treatment. That was the only way for him to save her. Swetanka! Is it not dedication? But you are callous towards your family. What has happened to you? I haven't heard of any person, absorbed in literature, becomes so much detached and exclusivist. Tell me, what has actually happened ? Are you really irresponsible and indifferent?"

Reading Sarat's letter about his father's helplessness, he immediately returned to his residence from office sulking. But he was not at all perturbed by the words such as responsibility, thinking, etc. In fact, he was surprised as he felt suffering so intimately! How so much pain had got frozen in him, he wondered. And yet he was incapable of comprehending it! As if, there was nothing in the world to comprehend and the world does not run on understanding. Swetanka too didn't reply to Sarat. Perhaps man has lost his power of explaining himself to others since the day when he has been fascinated by the beauty of the world while trying to understand something. Consequently man forgot himself and got stupefied because of it. Swetanka questioned himself if he was irresponsible and indifferent and whether he had not shouldered any other responsibility than analyzing himself. He stumbled over such questions and was not able to move further. So what's possible thereafter was only struggling with the question. And that won't be a story since no story teller can be responsible for such question.

STORY 2

Are not you the same Swetanka? Do you still sport a thin moustache on your long face and have thick hair on eye-brows? Do you still smile at very small things? Do you still shout there loudly as you used to do while gathering children on festive days to visit fairs? Are you still arranging picnics there as you were doing here by collecting rice from door to door every month? When you would get angry, you go on fasting for two to three forenoons. You get pacified if and when I swear by my name. At times you would get angry deliberately just for my swearing. Am I right? Are you getting angry there also? Is there any one who swears like me? Are not you that Swetanka? I am confirmed from your demeanour that you don't have that attachment towards me any more. Even though I wrote to you every month, you haven't replied for the last six months. Moreover, I am also sure that not only to this Sudipa but also to any other Sudipa. I am confounded, how being a bachelor you remained unemotional even when you got letters from a girl! How did you become so indifferent? Have you met with any accident in your life or do you suffer from any inexpressible acute pain? What has happened to you?

I have asked you similarly several times. And my questions have returned to me as answers. Do you know sister Sanju has became an ascetic? Are you really concerned about her? Aren't you her brother? Perhaps you aren't bothered about her marriage. When asked she says, "I know father and my younger brother are unable to give me in marriage. I also failed to arrange it myself because I felt terribly nervous. I apprehended I might be deceived. Similarly, I couldn't elope with someone just for prestige of the family. I do no more harbour that sort of attitude now. What more to do? Yes, my asceticism is a mere pretension, a sort of acting yet it is a shelter too." Heard her Swetanka! Is this not sister Sanju's sacrifice for your family?"

Till now Swetanka has listened to stories about suffering and sacrifice as though human civilization were replete with their histories! As if nothing were possible without these! May be, these stories have unnerved and weakened him. Whereever you cast your eyes, you find sufferings and sacrifices, then why so much indulgence in life? Why so much depravity? Swetanka feels perplexed and simply stares. He musters no courage to question anybody about these. He feels none is his neighbour, all strangers!

STORY 3

Swetanka manages to get the post of a clerk with much strain and bribery of two thousand rupees. He never considers bribery to be as such; takes it easy. He thinks our civilization has not stooped to such level rather the yardstick of our national life is attached to it. At the time of bribing, he asked if it could be spared. The reply was, "Aren't you fortunate to get a job when thousands of young men remain unemployed? It's better, you think you were unemployed and will remain so six more months. That's all. Salary for six months is only two thousand rupees."

Swetanka thought so, though it was painful for him. How can one evade a compelling thought in a compelling century? He turned more pensive the day he got the job and was serious not to lose it, come what may. Very difficult indeed to get a job in a country of unemployment and more difficult than this is how to sustain it. Because he felt as if a conspiracy to snatch it away from him encircled him always! Hence he remained shaky and petrified for four years in service. He turned more afraid and felt like bleeding.

It was mid March. At its end, all members of staff would be paid their arrears and travelling allowance too. They did not get their T.A. every month due to lack of govt. sanction and would be paid at this time. But some trouble surfaced for fixation of percentage. It's a habitual fact. The officer would say, "I won't approve tour diaries unless I am paid twenty percent. Why shall I do it in gratis? All your tour diaries are false. So, I shall approve sixteen to seventeen daily allowances per month if you pay me twenty percent. Since I am the drawing and disbursing officer, I am responsible for all this. Why should not I take percentage?"

In this connection, treasury was far above as it would take seven percent. Clerks in a treasury would wash their mouth with money in March. At this hurry and crucial moment all Treasury Rules and regulations against this would be flouted. Hundreds of bills would be prepared burning midnight oil towards the end of March. So, there must be some mistakes! They will attach an objection slip if they are not paid percentage. Then money cannot be drawn. Hence seven percent must be paid with due humility without playing with the treasury. Then arose the problem of the concerned bill clerk and accountant in the office. The accountant would claim twenty percent. Why should I pass the bill without percentage? He would whine. Office of the head of the department would swallow ten percent to send allotment; the clerk at the treasury would take seven percent just to ok it; the officer concerned would pocket twenty percent to sign blindly; and why would we prepare your bills sweating day and night for nothing? We are more responsible for this for all will escape if any trouble arises afterwards but we two will be under fire. We won't allow that to happen and won't prepare your bill unless we are paid twenty percent. Let us see how you could draw your T.A.

In the aggregate all this come to fifty-seven percent. The field staff were annoyed and they felt, though they were the heart of all governmental work, they were dictated terms by all. That led to bickering, manhandling and fisticuffs. Even letters of complaint were also written. At this critical stage Swetanka shouldered all responsibility and turned mediator. He realized that it was March, a rich harvesting month for all; month of their monetary gain. So he did not bother for morality and tried to bargain with the officer, accountant, staff, and treasury clerk. His clever mediation worked. He solved the problem with thirty-five percent only. Even beneficiaries cheered him as their leader and he was blown sky-high. Contented, they said, "The boy is not only intellectual but also has acumen to be a leader. But for him, we could not have got T. A. this year."

But Swetanka felt terribly hurt because of this. He shuddered as he brooded, " Alas! How fallen I am! How rotten collective consciousness today is! These people can heap accolades on one even if one compromises on immorality!" Then he turned impassive, though got annoyed inside. He didn't feel sad for his mediation but felt deeply as all proclaimed him to be a very important person. At last he told aloud, "Whatever it may be, I consider it to be a hideous misdeed. Hence I won't accept any percentage even though I am bill clerk." All got struck dumb with his expression but did not desist from submitting bills. Rather they remarked, "Rubbish. He does not run short of money. Even he spends more than sixty rupees per month on purchasing magazines. So why should he salivate for percentage? But we must deduct ten percent for you too, whether you take it or not."

Now Swetanka realized such collective strategy to kill a person's character by means of collective service.

LAST STORY; ENDLESS

Irritated, Swetanka thought sadly that his refusal of such percentage was only for his economic strength-his friend considered. Though at times, he didn't have a single pie in his pocket to purchase an envelope to send his story to a magazine a week after he received his monthly emolument. Silently he returned to his residence.

At his residence he found his sugar jar filled with swarms of ants. The ants were reigning over the entire house as it were! They, in single file, were moving with sugar on their face. He had opened the jar in the morning to bring sugar to eat with flattened rice and forgotten to seal it tightly. The ants took advantage of it. Swetanka crushed them with his legs as if to avenge the irritation he had swallowed in the office. Even he did not spare any of them. But what about the ants who were already inside the jar? He poured the sugar swarmed with ants on a piece of news paper and held the ants one by one in his hands. He was seething with annoyance. But it was very difficult, almost impossible, to crush all the ants separating them one by one. They ran, got scattered almost all over. He was pulling them with his finger. They were running here and there fearfully. He felt exhausted and impatient even to crush the ants!

Out of excessive irritation he poured the sugar mixed with ants into the jar and tightly put its lid- "You bloody fool, what will you do now? Get asphyxiated", he fumed.

From outside the jar, he saw the ants inside were unconcerned about their death, engrossed in collecting grains of sugar. Swetanka sported a devilish laughter, kept the jar in the usual place and moved to the town on bicycle.

Eyes bedimmed with faded stars, he left the field empathetically. Wretched ants- he thought emotionally as milk of human kindness streamed down in him. What's the fault of ants? What solution had he got by killing them amass? The culture of pain and dedication has kept him very impassive so far. His father, sister Sanju , friend Sarat, beloved Sudipa, brother Rohit, and, above all, his job, all are good as they were previously. But why did the ants die? What for?

Now Swetanka realised- a creature does not turn inanimate even after death. No not at all. He gets frightened when he finds a dead snake or dead frog in front of his bicycle. He can't run the bicycle over them as he feels something inside. He feels as though these creatures long dead were most lively. They are lively till their last existence. Mercy cascaded in Swetanka's story. The story can't be stopped. It will run spontaneously. The dry leaf in his shirt pocket was still intact.

Upset lock, stock and barrel, he ran his bicycle towards his residence. Unlocking the door, he switched on light, picked up the jar in a hurry and looked into it intently. But where were the ants? He was struck with wonder. After close scrutiny he found them dead together in a corner of the jar. Swetanka screamed with inconceivable pain. While alive, the ants were moving here and there inside the glass jar but went into a huddle in a corner of the jar to die. Swetanka could not fathom its mystery. He was nonplussed. An impenetrable mystery of the Creation,it turned more mysterious before him. It appeared as though Sartre,

Camus, Kafka, Ionesco and Faulkner- all were defeated because of the ant's demeanour!. Was it that the ants could foresee their death and therefore embraced it gleefully hugging each other?

Swetanka could think no more. All he had previously thought compulsorily became trifling before him. Silently he shed tears for the dead ants. He poured them with sugar on a piece of paper and found to his astonishment that even the dead ants didn't fall scattered. They fell on the ground as a lump as though they were in tight embrace still. Swetanka pulled out the dry leaf from his pocket, put the dead ants on it and paddled his bicycle towards the river bank.

Solitude everywhere. Only murmurs of the moon-blanched river were being heard. At times flutter of the Baya weaver birds from the nearby palm tree and jackal's hooting sounded. Swetanka made the dry leaf with the dead ants on it drift in the river and said, " Drifting all along when you reach the unknown zone, you will say that you all alone did not go there, you had plucked the dry leaf from Swetanka!"

While returning he decided he would go to his village next morning on seven days' leave.

Gendua

At the approach of dusk when conch shells sounded, a rickshaw horn blew at the outer side of the bamboo gate, and then Gendua stammered: Open the gate !

Pachi, his third wife came out lighting a lamp; two kids followed her. The elder Buddhi blew the horn of the rickshaw twice while Gendua pushed it through the gate elatedly and asked, "O, Gendua, have you brought me the crispy cake?"

- Shut up! You address me by my first name as if you were my father! Gendua retorted while locking the rickshaw. He handed over a bag of rice, a small phial of mustard oil and a polythene bag of fish and then rested himself on the verandah while wiping sweat. As Pachi went inside the house with the bag, Gendua beckoned his three year old son Noka. The child came and he dangled a cake before him and said: I shall give you this. But tell me who I am ?

: Gendua! The child babbled.

Gendua's anger rose high and he raised his hand to beat him. But he contained himself with a hush. Then he murmured. A while later he picked him to his lap, gave him the cake and asked, "Tell, who I am."

- Gendua! The child replied. Gendua threw him on the ground and flared up, "Rubbish, bloody bastard, learns nothing". Then he went to the tank to wash himself. The children ran to Pachi tearfully. Returning he asked his wife if tea was ready.

-Oh, yes, just a minute. You forgot to bring sugar. I have added molasses to tea. I am bringing it soon.

Gendua kept mum leaning against a bamboo pole. To alleviate his leg pain, he massaged himself. Since his wife was busy, how could she massage him until domestic duties were over!

Darkness deepened. Bats were fluttering around the front neem tree. Gendua sipped a cup of raw tea placed before him by his wife and cogitated with a sense of despair: "How long can people like us survive with only such tea in the morning and evening and with lunch and dinner half-fed? Restless labour day and night, right from the age of seven to thirty, devours your health, longevity, all your physical stamina gets sapped and all your labour is limited. Just one keeps one's body and soul together. Alas! in spite of hard labour since my seventh year, I have remained ill-fed throughout. How can one rear zest for living? Even though one's belief in work gets shattered, one can't escape from the belief in God so easily. Once it is uprooted, it is tantamount to committing suicide. Yes, one has to strive hard to keep this belief burning."

Gendua continued sipping tea while swimming in the sea of despair. The sound of Buddhi and Noka's munching the crispy cake came from his house. He heard someone opening the gate and coming inside. He stood up in awe. He knew not why he was afraid of human beings these days. His thirty years' experience climaxed only in fearing human beings.

"Well, are not you Gendua standing there?" A strange voice asked. Gendua was surprised beyond measure as he saw Bhajaharibabu, owner of his rickshaw. How come he was there! If occasion demanded, he would send his servant Giria with a taunting instruction to him "Go, get that bloody bastard stammerer here".

Gendua greeted him politely, requesting him to come in.

- No, no, I was just here on a work. I saw the rickshaw. Why have n't you paid yesterday's due?

- Sir, I shall pay it next morning, Gendua replied.

- All right, are you tired? Didn't you pull the rickshaw tonight? Bhajahari asked in a tone of despondency.

- No, Sir, feeling unwell, headache.

- Well, let us see tomorrow the hood of the rickshaw is repaired. But what about your rehearsal with your kids, teaching them to address you as "Father"?

Gendua extended a constrained laughter in order to avoid such an awkward question. Then Bhajaharibabu left the place.

To be addressed as father, who does not want? Gendua's eyes shone in darkness, his heart pounding in despair. Ah! Fatherhood is everybody's desire.

'Struggle for existence - its root is fatherhood. All your sweat and blood leads to the root of fatherhood.

This country addressed Mahatma Gandhi as Bapu; Marx was regarded as the messiah of the down trodden, Ambedkar was hailed as father of the Indian Constitution; Sarala Das, the great was called father of Odia Literature. To exert fatherhood is man's eternal proclivity and coronation of his manliness. The history of paternity is the yardstick of human civilization. So much struggle for and so much pursuit of politics, science, religion and literature is only to acquire paternity. Continuous expansion of DNA is concealed in paternity. And, the flow of generation is the eternal existence of one's aspiration. What is more, God Himself is the Universal Father. Hence, who does not desire paternity?'

Gendua is so abjectly hapless always that he has not been fortunate to listen to the sonorous call of "father". Even though he has been goading Buddhi and Noka to call him father, he has not heard such much awaited call from them.

He could see the face of his father Mathuri that shone in pitch darkness as he was seized with the emotion of paternity in his heart. His face twitched.

Though Gendua was a stammerer and dwarf he was adventurous in his childhood. He could climb big and tall palm trees to pluck tender palm fruits and swim along fathomless river streams to reach the other shore. His mother passed away when he was only five. Thenceforth he was getting motherly touch in the spontaneous lap of nature. Though his father didn't marry again, he turned promiscuous, as they said. For that he was insulted mercilessly when caught red-handed. Sometimes his face was smeared with black colour, sometimes his buttocks were branded with a hot sickle. And somewhere he was fined too. When eighteen, his father got him married to a tall, buxom girl, older than him by four to five years. And he told his villagers, "Son of bitch, climbing trees. He may fall off tree one day and die. I have brought him a plump woman; he may ride her as much as he desires."

No doubt, he brought a daughter in law for his son but both would be satisfied - the villagers took to rumours.

Mathuri got irritated with Gendua after about three months of the marriage. He commented,"Lo, our son is pampering his wife while his father is labouring hard. Sons nowadays go to Assam, Kolkata or any colliery for earnings which they send to their parents every month after keeping their body and soul together. But you bloody fool, why are you whiling away time at home?"

Gendua journeyed to Kolkota in company of Nainda Sahoo as he could not put up with his father's irritation always. At Kolkota he carried water to different houses, earned and sent money to his father every month. But he always felt homesick. As 'Raja festival' drew near he was quite overwhelmed with emotion to go home. He purchased a piece of saree, some bangles, blouse, scented oil, etc. for his wife and was homeward. As he reached the outskirts of the village, some villagers dolefully said, "Hello boy, why did you return? What will you find at your home? Your wife is no more yours; she has already become your stepmother. Go and see."

Gendua felt nonplussed, his eyes sunk deep and his countenance stooped- "Is he my father or a monster?" He mumbled with a heavy heart. When his feet touched his village with all gaiety, he turned tired. "Father! Why did not you marry again if you were still sexually starved? I would not have protested. Even you could have married Sabi and I would have prostrated before her. But what did you do? A man of fifty, you thought none will give you his daughter in marriage. So you committed such a shameful act"- he thought burning in anger.

However, he proceeded towards his house silently, thinking the villagers might be spreading a rumour. There were his enemies in the village. They might be doing so. The sun was setting by degrees. The nulla near the village was filled with muddy water. A pack of herons were fluttering in the sky. He reached home and felt annoyed with Sabi's behaviour.

- Son, I would have written to you tomorrow to come

for the 'Raja' festival. You did a very good thing as you came of your own accord, said father Mathuri.

Sabi served him a very sumptuous dinner with so many items gleefully and with sprightly words. The sky got clouded and it began raining torrentially in no time. Lightning flashed again and again. Gendua was beside himself with joy, thinking whatever he heard from the villagers was false. It was just a conspiracy to denigrate his family. After all, his father was his father. Nursing any doubt against him was sinful, he cautioned himself. The night advanced while Sabi entered her bedroom. Gendua was simply turning sides in his bed. Sabi bolted the room from inside spraying smiles.

Gendua woke up at the dead of night. No rain in the sky. He groped around his bed, but where was Sabi! The door was open. The spear of his doubt got sharpened, while his chest burnt.

-O, God, pray Thee, let my doubt not be true. I could not bear if it is so. Like a thief he stealthily came out of the room, his throat parching. He overheard near his father's bedroom, his father's words and the sounds of bangles- "Go, now. Before Gendua wakes up, go to him."

Gendua's suspicion turned true, his eyes becoming bloodshot; his world well lost. Filial relationship denoted by the creature called father died in his mind. Filled with utter dejection he stumbled to his bed. Not a wink of sleep he had. How could there be sleep when the zephyr of heart born of slumber turned into hot air? Like a newly wed wife, Sabi entered his room and after bolting the door she slept beside him.

- You bloody bitch, prostitute! Gendua soundlessly reiterated. In the morning he left home and returned drinking country liquor. Then he started beating his father and wife, snarling "Are you my father or monster"? If you were sexually so much excited, why did not you marry her? Why did you destroy my life ? You bloody bitch; you failed to distinguish between husband and father in law. Get out of this house. If I see you here again, I will tear you into pieces." Gendua screamed.

The entire village crowded his house. As Sabi was beaten black and blue, she ran to her father's house. Gendua also left for Kolkata, vowing not to see this father again. His father was bedridden being beaten by his son ruthlessly. He was ridiculed by the villagers contemptuously. Ultimately he died lamenting his son. Gendua returned to his village. He cultivated his three acres of land himself and led a luxurious life. So many marriage proposals were offered to him but he declined. He said straightway - No question of marrying again!

Sabi's memory made him spit against womankind, yet at night he could hear the tinkling sound of Sabi's bangles; he also felt the absence of her warm breasts on his chest and was disappointed. A few days later his uncle Shankar arranged a girl for him and insisted that he married her. Gendua agreed without murmur. The marriage was solemnized. But three months after his marriage, when he came to know that his second wife was pregnant for six months, whatever faith he had, got swamped in the limbo of darkness. He scolded his uncle and bade goodbye to his wife. "Libido is the root of all evils, hence it must be heavily dealt with. It must be nipped in the bud". Deciding so, he visited the nearby health center and underwent vasectomy. He thought sexual desire won't crop up because of such operation. No phallus, no desire.

But his villagers reprimanded him saying, 'Man's aspirations, dreams centre round the desire for creating progeny. What did you fool do! You have not yet fathered a child and you castrated yourself !"

Gendua did not pay any heed to their comments and retorted, "I have done the right thing. The two women I married are sexually immoral. So what faith should I have?" But when he realized that the operation had deceived him, he felt terribly restless. Such operation would prevent his fatherhood but it won't be able to shut the window of desire and necessity of woman. Alas! Who would give him his daughter in marriage now!

As time rolled on the hapless Gendua went on crying bitterly and wandered here and there like a lunatic. His world was well lost, he couldn't become a father. Now he was alone; he became callous to work, sold his landed property. The village touts embezzled him and bought his remaining landed property at a throwaway price. He was left only with his paternal dwelling. He was awfully worried, how to keep his body and soul together! Undone, he hired someone's rickshaw and pulled it to eke out his living. One summer day he had been to Santarapur with passengers in his rickshaw. Very hot air was splashing in the late afternoon. He couldn't return and took shelter in an old woman's house.

The old woman had a widowed daughter, Pachi by name. Mother of two children, she didn't get two square meals a day. Though a widow, Pachi was still young and the colour of her body was quite captivating. In course of talk, the old woman narrated her weal and woe. Gendua too told her to accept Pachi as his wife and be father of her children. The old woman agreed. That's all. Birds of hope and delight started flying in Gendua's sky. He brought home Pachi and her children in his rickshaw. The villagers passed adverse comments - How funny, you brought both the cow and her calves together! All right! It would be nice if you are addressed as father! It's doubtful; the woman won't live with you as you have undergone vasectomy. Be cautious, not to open prostitution in this hamlet.

Gendua fell out with him who remarked this way and stopped talking to him too. In fact, Pachi was in dark about Gendua's operation. But when she knew she felt shocked. Then she consoled herself that whatever might be the case, at least she and her children would be taken care of. Moreover, her children would get a father. So, she kept mum. Gendua addressed her as Genduani (female Gendua) just to show her his allegiance as his wife. However, he started pulling the rickshaw at night time just to hide his inability for fatherhood.

"What can I do? The owner of the rickshaw gives to somebody else at day time and me at night. I am undone, he would tell his wife. Pachi too would remain silent.

Gendua returns very early in the morning, takes gruel rice and falls asleep. He takes rice in the afternoon again. At noon, he makes daughter Buddhi and son Noka sit beside him and with a cane in hand starts a rehearsal asking them, "Tell me, who am I? .... Your father, I am; call me father!" But, the children address him as 'Gendua'. This enrages him, so that he beats them urging them to call him father but to no avail. Dangling some crispy cake before them at times he would ask them to call him father but the children, after treating themselves with such cakes, still would call him by his first name.

No result would come out if you either beat or cajoled them. They would address you as father when they desired, said Pachi.

If they did not learn in childhood, what would happen when they grew up? Gendua would retort.

All his efforts were of no avail as Buddhi and Noka never addressed him as father.

As Baina, (another rickshaw puller) who used to pull the rickshaw at forenoon, didn't take rickshaw this morning, Gendua had to take it in the morning. Otherwise he used to pull it at night time. Taking this advantage did Bhajahari Babu visit his home at night? He questioned himself.

Turning into a tortoise in deep darkness, as it were, Gendua heaved a deep sigh in unspeakable affliction and went inside his house drawing his stick from the roof. Buddhi and Noka were found munching a crispy cake while Pachi was scaling a fish.

Raising the stick, he asked Buddhi – 'Tell me, who has brought you this crispy cake?'

Gendua, she replied.

The same question and the same answer by Noka infuriated him. He thrashed them many times saying, "O God, my life is rotten".

As Buddhi and Noka cried bitterly, Pachi scolded him angrily, "Don't pose yourself to be father. Are your competent to be so?"

This silenced him, he had no answer to Pachi's question. Hence he withdrew himself to the front verandah of the house where he became a part of darkness. It would be better if he could vanish in darkness, he went on thinking. Pachi had already known about his impotence. Buddhi and Noka didn't call him father even after much rehearsal and entreat. "Maybe this woman, taking advantage of my night duty, would be offering herself somewhere outside. If so, why should I labour for their livelihood? Why should I shoulder their responsibility?" He remained awfully anxiety-ridden for some days.

At about midnight one day, while he was returning home with his empty rickshaw along the National highway, a gentleman called him in a dark square. Gendua halted. Pointing at a woman standing at a little distance, the gentleman said, "Drive this woman to Minapur; I shall give you ten rupees."

Gladly he agreed as Minapur was his native village. He would get ten rupees and he won't have to return, he felt exultant.

The gentleman gave him ten rupees and the woman boarded the rickshaw, covering her face with her saree. Gendua's rickshaw rolled towards Minapur. He didn't talk with her lest she would feel otherwise as she was alone. As they approached Minapur, he asked, "Whose house you want to go to?

The woman remained silent. Gendua repeated the question politely.

- Let us go! She said gently. Gendua's eyes bulged, O! it was Pachi's voice.

His feet on the pedal became immobile. He felt he would be mad. What's the affair the lady involved in? She had already opened her trade even on the highway! Gendua trembled in anger.

He did not know how and when he reached the gate of his house with a heart ruffled in a tsunami and the roving eyes of a dejected bird. In a state of indifference, he opened the gate and entered.

A wicker lamp was burning. Noka and Buddhi just then sobbing inconsolably on the verandah, ran towards him, clasped him and cried more bitterly, saying 'Father! Mother has deserted us.'

Gendua was excited. As he came to his senses, he felt innumerable jasmines had blossomed in the deep dark night, as it were. He took Buddhi and Noka to his lap. Tears rolled down his cheeks.

- Father, where is mother? Buddhi queried. Stealthily Pachi walked towards the house. She stayed put with a tinge of surprise.

A Circus

Eva crouched in an A/C room in the third storey. Eleven o'clock. The scorching sun scourged while dry, biting wind lashed all around.

She surveyed the road and the scene of the town burning. She peered through the upper part of the window pane and saw a five storied building was in progress. A long bamboo platform had been erected for this. Taken aback, she rang the calling bell. In came Sankari, almost of her age in the wrong side of fifty. Yet she didn't use glasses while Eva had been using it for the last ten years. Though her housemaid for eight years, Shankari was exclusively her maid. She knew Eva's past and present and was able to read her on her visage. In good faith, Eva too had unravelled her being, almost all her secrets to her.

Now Shankari marked a pendulum of surprise swinging on Eva's face. She looked here and there but failed to decipher. Eva looked through the window again and said, "Well, look, look at a little distance."

Shankari did as bidden and saw passersby walking along the road. The hoardings looked like unseen oceanic creatures. No unusual or attractive scene or object caught her eyes. So, she beamed with query.

-Saw the circus? Eva asked.

-Where ? Shankari fumbled as she cast her glance here and there.

-How come you fail to see? A five - storied building is under construction. A woman with bricks on a wooden plank on her head climbs a long bamboo ladder. Can't you see it? Eva said.

As Shankari peered, her countenance turned pale. She said, 'Yes, I saw. A woman labourer is labouring for wages. It's not circus, but labour'.

In a fit of excitement, Eva expressed, "Is it possible to labour in such scorching sun? She must have drugged herself."

She is bound to labour in such a condition.

Hunger has no season, Whether summer or rain. It persists.

Eva looked here and there. Her eyes got stuck to the window pane. Maybe she got a little sign. Turning her face, she looked at Shankari in askance. This frightened Shankari and encouraged her as well. She looked searchingly and smiled after a while.

Why smiling? Eva asked.

-Your object of surprise is the butt of my smile'- replied Shankari.

To gauge Shankari's intelligence, Eva turned quizzical and asked "Tell me regarding the object !"

Shankari smiled and said, "That woman's bulging belly. She is pregnant. Yet she climbs so high up the ladder with weighty bricks on her head. Isn't it?"

-Exactly ! Astonishment still writ large on her face, Eva expressed.

-She is habituated - Shankari clarified it like the demarcation line of powder used in a kitchen against ants and cockroaches.

-O God! I now remember the news of my first pregnancy from the doctor. It made me happy though I trembled in fear devastatingly and asked my father to appoint a nurse. You were not at that time. An experienced nurse guarded me day and right. But that woman ... Eva broke in the middle and got stuck to the window pane again. In a dazed state she started, "Look Shankari! How the woman, brick on her head and child in her womb, climbs the ladder higher and higher so easily! Just as we enter the Paradise Garden at five o' clock." Eva turned her face and Shankari heaved deeply.

-My head reels as I see the circus, said Eva.
No circus, Madam, it is labour.

Let it be. Draw the curtain. I feel benumbed, my eyes getting drawn.

Shankari obeyed. And Eva stretched herself on the bed.

It was evening that day. Eva was rocking in her garden swing. Shankari ran to her, completely pallid and said, "Madam, that woman died. The pregnant woman we saw carrying bricks on her head and climbing the bamboo ladder used for construction of the five storied - building! You remember? She fell down and succumbed to death with the child in her womb.

Shankari felt like babbling due to emotion. Her eyes appeared to mark some change on Eva's face and drew some sympathetic expression from her.

Still Eva was rocking in the swing, stroking her hair. Shankari felt ill at ease and insulted too. Time wore on.

-What's that to me? Why tell me about that? Eva expressed nonchalantly.

Shankari stumbled. Eva's question was a slap on her cheeks.

-Madam, I told you because you felt emotional at her climbing higher on a ladder with bricks on her head in the day time, she said haltingly.

Still Eva continued swinging and stroking her hair. Well, that was an amazing circus at that time, said Eva.

- No circus, but labour,
- No circus, but labour!

Shankari tried to spell it out ten thousand times but could not. As though, someone shut her mouth!

Bees were humming in the garden; butterflies whirling around.

Shankari said again, "Madam, A big bazaar is going to be opened in that five storied building."

Is it? Eva asked hilariously and continued, "A very good piece of information. But do you know when it opens?"

Shankari felt guilty as she had not collected such information. Indeed, she was good for nothing. Collecting such information was much more important than the news of the death of the pregnant woman labourer!

Still swinging, Eva said, "Well, go and prepare coffee for me. I am sure; some Bollywood star must grace the ceremony. And I must be invited."

No more did she speak. She rocked onward and backward. Shankari did not think it proper to be there anymore. She left to prepare coffee.

In that aggressive summer evening the Elephant Mall sparkled. Eva loitered from shop to shop in Shankari's company. The mall was air-conditioned altogether. They stood on the escalator to go upstairs. The stairs were moving. Eva was on the stair before Shankari. As the escalator touched the upstairs'-floor Eva failed to pass immediately as her shoes got stuck. She was thrown upon the upstair floor. Shankari jumped in no time. Eva was wounded. Some persons rushed to her. Eva got up and said, "Thanks, I am least affected. I was just unmindful!"

Those persons returned. Eva tried to study herself. The mall looked ablaze again. Shankari said eloquently, "Just as circus!"

Eva's eyes burned in anger. She said, "Do you feel this to be a circus when my knees are aching? I may not be able to walk. Let us visit an orthopaedic doctor."

- Lucky you are. Shankari expressed with a deep sigh.

- What do you mean?

- Look. This building was under construction. The woman was climbing the bamboo ladder carrying bricks on her head in scorching heat. She was pregnant too .... Shankari didn't complete the sentence intentionally and gazed at Eva's face intently.

- Yes, I saw that circus. You informed me later that the woman died. Eva stopped abruptly. The scene of the pregnant woman carrying bricks in stinging summer, fallings off a bamboo ladder and getting blooded got intensified in her. She massaged her aching knee, screaming.

■

The Slaughter

Kalu continued running rashly, shouting 'it's devouring'. Stunned, the passerby looked at him. Kalu was running along the main road of the town tirelessly with almost breathless ejaculations – 'O! I am dying, dying, it's eating me out !' The twenty- year- old robust Kalu was running, and running. Magu, his old father, at his heels was equally impatient, shouted-'O Kalu! Please wait, proceed not.' Their unusual race stirred the bystanders beside the road to know of its cause.

Magu's meat shop was at the Badabazar square. Every morning he used to proceed to the place with knife, chopper, basket, plates made of sal leaves and plantain leaves. Kalu followed him dragging half a dozen of goats tied to a piece of rope. When bleating of the goats would turn the entire road lachrymose, his eyes registered a note of pathos; his heart getting wet in emotion. Though he was habituated with this meat business since his childhood he felt the bleating of goats as of execution of earth. He used to yoke them to a bamboo post near the cabin and place banyan leaves before their mouth. Were they aware of the cruel tragedy that would befall them after a while? He had heard some opined that the goat-ascetic was born to maintain a social balance of man's greed for meat and cruelty thereof. At Mother Kali's behest, a saint in goat form would be born time and again; and being butchered it would save human society from the sense of guilt. Man has contrived religious, spiritual, and social alibis galore to hide his brutal deviation.

Alas! Even man has treated the animal of his prey as a symbol of cruelty. Kalu has heard many such arguments from the buyers that frequent his shop and is taken aback with such type of man's attitude. He has failed to understand why man is not straight about his carnivorousness; why he does not frankly say that he kills the animal for this ? Moreover, he has heard some buyers saying – the goat slaughterer attains heaven; he takes unto himself all the sins of the butchered goat. Thereby, sacredness accrues to him because he frees the goat from its sins. Also he has heard someone saying: the butcher does not kill the goat as long as its owner bids him to take it to finish. As a result, he is not afflicted by sin.

This morning Kalu dragged two goats to the abattoir. He looked at their eyes silently and searchingly after fastening them to the post near the cabin. He perceived no death in those eyes but the butcher's knife. He closed his eyes. Buyers were already there.

- Ah, what succulent goats today! Not at all diseased. Well, where is Magu ? Why so late ? One of them asked.

With a knife and plates made of leaves in hand Magu came. "Go and get the big one butchered" he ordered Kalu.

Kalu failed to obey his bidding and kept mum. Angrily Magu flung vituperative words at him, "You bloody fool, why sitting still? Take the big one. Practise the work from today. You are already matured. When will you learn the trade? Finish it soon."

Kalu's eyes got widened; he never thought he would butcher goats like his father. He has scaled skin, chopped legs of the goat butchered, slashed its heart to pieces;

measured meat and sold. But he never did butchery. So, he felt unnerved beyond measure as he heard what his father bade; as though he was dragged to be butchered ! Not a word did he utter; he sat motionless.

An old buyer said, "Hello boy, when Magu was of your age, he was being requisitioned to butcher seven to eight goats daily. So, do it now as the old man is no more able to do it."

Still Kalu was unmoved. If he started butchering goats today, he would continue to be a butcher throughout life. But he didn't appreciate such life, he thought. Kalu's silence infuriated Magu more and he said, "You son of bitch, away, away. How long will you depend on this old man? You have been involved in this trade very often. Yet, you are so cowardly! Do you feel slaughtering goat sinful? If there were no fish eaters there would be no fisherman. Even if we stop slaughtering goat, every family will give birth to such slaughterers. Understand?"

Then the old man turned grave. The buyers' eyes salivated. Mustering courage, Kalu held a knife and with a fleshy goat entered the place of butchery at the rear of the cabin. He strengthened his trembling heart and tied the goat entirely. The goat bleated and lo, his eyes dimmed. His heart softened like a lump of mud. He placed the knife at the goat's throat though, he failed to pierce it. He was surprised. In fact, at a conscientious moment nobody can wound a goat, not to speak of killing it. Ah, man creates so many cruel moments in the world as and when he kills lakhs of creatures like goats, cocks, etc. As a result, he passes through so much cruel experience.

The goat was bleating nonstop. Knife in hand, Kalu sat in an overwhelming state. Harsh words of his father from this side stung him, "Kalu, are you butchering the goat or fondling it? Be courageous, strengthen your heart, harden your eyes and grip. Then things will be all right."

Now Kalu hardened himself. But unless cruelty swallows one's heart lock, stock and barrel, mere gnashing of teeth and tightening of grip will fall flat to commit butchery. It's not like chopping vegetables! How can one stab a goat unless one nurses hatred, anger, and violence against it? Moreover, one can't kill it so easily if one considers it to be an inanimate object or vegetable. As Magu shouted again he made himself firm. His eyes turned diabolical, teeth started gnashing and his grip became violent and his face cruel. He could see nothing all around. He held the throat of the goat, heeded not its bleating and cut its throat with the knife. In no time streams of blood spurted from the goat's throat resulting in its prolonged heart rending, bleating. Kalu let loose the goat's throat because of such sound. His eyes bulged too. Terribly petrified, he felt the bleeding goat rushing to bite him with vengeance.

Thereafter he shouted, time and again, 'O, it devours me, devours me' and ran. He ran like the wind followed by his father bidding him to stay and be patient. As Kalu crossed the Big Bazar, he saw a tradesman coming with more than two dozens of goats. He felt hundreds of bleating goats running towards him in unison, as it were. Kalu stayed put; he was frightened and desperate. As the goats approached him he felt as if they were about to attack him. His head reeled and he fell down unconscious. When he regained consciousness, he found himself sleeping in front of his cabin. His father was splashing water on his face while a lot of people had surrounded him. Magu's face turned grave and he said, "If you are nervous about this work at the beginning and fail thereby, then you are sure to fail throughout your life."

The goat was dead by that time due to heavy bleeding. Magu deposited the dead goat before Kalu and asked, "Well, were you not troubled by this goat?

- Yea, Kalu replied.

Magu handed over the knife and said, "Then finish it soon".

Kalu got apprehensive of the work and fainted. "Let him do this later."- a buyer said. Promptly Magu replied – 'Sir, if he does not get rid of fear, he will be more cowardly. Killing of a goat is not potato chopping.'

Then he said to Kalu in a tremulous voice, "Slice its neck into two. Be quick!"

Kalu held the dead goat's neck in his left hand and put the knife in his right hand there. Yet he was indisposed, had no inclination to slice. He closed his eyes and gnashed his teeth.

- I have brought you for business, not to rear you, or stroke you in affection. You are not my pal, or relation. My prey you are." Thus saying, he felt his heart getting bolder. Instantly the knife in his hand pierced the goat's neck.

- Well done my son- Magu patted him on his back.

As Kalu opened his eyes, he saw the goat's head rolling in two pieces.

- "Killing a goat is not that difficult. One can do it if one keeps one's heart, eyes, hands and grip strong and thinks that one is a meat trader"- he thought.

The Land Of The Queen
Of Leftovers

Midday. Jhankuli asked her eldest son Makar to unbutton his pant; as it tightened his belly; then gulped the pudding. She told her youngest son Chachar, "Well, here is a fried piece of fish, eat it." Handing the plate containing potato roast over to her youngest daughter Saun, she said, -"Take it, mix dal with rice and take it with these. Finish the leftovers of the rice boiled with meat and ghee."

Jhankuli wiped the least amount of the red sauce in the glass plate with her finger and testing it she uttered "Ah!" She salivated and started licking the plate.

: A new thing indeed! She said.

Then she hurled a volley of abuses at her children-You damned scoundrels! Why don't you finish soon? Hi, Makar! Finish the spicy fry of lady'sfinger; and you Chchar! How is it you have not yet touched parwal- gravy? My dear Saun, swallow the spinach-curry, paneer soon. Hello Makar, you too have not taken that one! Chachar! You gulp that sweet and lick the plate. So tasty you know! Besides, so many other items are there-fish, prawn, egg, so on and so forth; you bloody fool children, finish it all soon."

Suddenly a tall girl in white uniform appeared there. Her piercingly indignant look silenced Jhankuli and she looked down. The girl scolded her mildly- Didn't I forbid you to use such filthy language here? Utter again and you will lose your job!

Jhankuli turned silent. Her three children stared in fear. After a while they became normal when their mother asked them to finish. Seventeen items of curry, they finished it to the lees. Only a handful of rice remained. Jhankuli spread the hem of her sari, placed a piece of palm leaf on it and wrapped that rice in it.

-This much for supper, she said. Then she went to the water tap with utensils to wash. The tall girl heaped there cooking pans, vessels, plates, etc. and ordered her to wash all well. Jhankuli looked at her helplessly as she found so many pieces of utensils. But she lowered her eyes the moment that girl stared at her.

She opened the tap, kept the utensils under its stream. She expressed her annoyance when the girl departed- "Hell with this. Can one person do this ?"

However, she called out her children, "You bastards! Be here forthwith and wash the utensils; I am washing the big vessels."

Suddenly the girl in white appeared before her and said- "You uttered the same filthy language again! Don't you feel ashamed as you scold your children in such language? Damn! you are almost dismissed from your job, you know!"

It made Jhankuli silent; she looked at her children in tearful eyes and busied herself washing the pans. The girl in white cast a spiteful glance at her. Jhankuli soliloquised, "You rogues! You begot children through me and fled; now I am finished!" She loved her children more than her life; the word 'rogues' that she used was not for them but against their fathers. Even such a word gushed forth spontaneously out of her as a token of protest and hatred against the illegal behaviour of the entire male folk .

For so many generations they have been living on the remnants of the royal family in exchange for washing utensils. Their wages were remnants of food. It had become a tradition. Many generations back, the generous king of the dynasty, on finding such huge amount of remnant food in shining utensils, had thought, "Why waste so much delicious curry day by day, rather it should be given away to families starving for days together? Hence, the remnant stuff after breakfast, dinner, evening snacks and supper should not be wasted. Let some families be appointed to utilise it. They would wash utensils to deserve such remnant food stuff." It was not simply an ordinary order, it was a royal one!

Thereafter Jhankuli's forefathers were appointed to such royal service. She inherited that infamous chapter of human history.

The dynasty waned like the moon after a full moon night. As the British left the country, kingship vanished. Yet its pomp and pride persisted. Hence, some families like that of Jhankuli still wallowed in such menial service. Such families were butt of humiliation every now and then. Even they were branded as "leftover eaters!" For such humiliation, her younger brother left the town. Nobody knows where he went. Her neighbour always teased her- "Fie, it is better to take poison than taking leftovers. I feel like belching the moment I think of it."

Jhankuli was about forty; she was habituated with taking leftovers with her mother here. And also she was washing utensils in its exchange. In those days people were afraid of her family since they were linked with the royal family. Rather they were anxious to establish bond with her. Even they used to talk with her unasked. But now they sneered when they saw her. In fact, Jhankuli was also no longer fond of taking leftovers. Yet she was diffident to get rid of such a humiliating job of washing utensils. Nor was she successful in preventing her children from this. Another problem she now faced. She did not know cooking as she had been depending on leftovers. In emergency, she would manage herself by begging food. Now she was apprehensive, very much perturbed for her children, because she was ridiculed as leftovers eater and her children would be addressed more abusively if they contiued with this. Moreover, at times the leftovers by the royal family was not enough. However, the motherly queen was gracious enough to leave some extra amount of rice, dal and curry for them on the dish. It would fill their belly. But a day might come when they won't get wages according to their labour. Whom would she complain then against this?

It was already dusk. Jhankuli was returning home followed by her three noisy children. All on a sudden a motor bike screeched to a halt just behind her. She was petrified. A tall bespectacled, fair- complexioned semi-old man in chudidar panjabi, dangling a golden chain around his neck and sporting a beard said "Well, were you frightened? I have some matters to talk to you. I am not a tiger or bear, come closer." Though she was afraid of such expression, she came near his bike in fearful eyes.

-Listen to me attentively; you and your children are engaged in washing utensils of the royal family. In exchange, you are getting meager leftovers. Give up such habit henceforth. Do you agree to work in a hotel, wash utensils there and get salary for that? Think of this throughout the night. Meet me here tomorrow at this hour and speak your mind - the man said.

Thereafter he left. Jhankuli felt springy. The life she had

dismissed as drab, dreary, almost a curse now appeared to be quite fascinating. She decided to leave her job with the royal family because managers of the royal family were uglier, more mischievous. Even after her eldest son Makar's birth, that rascal groom dared ask her what name she gave her son.

She remembered, she replied, "Not yet, but I shall give him the name Bikram."

This made him enraged and he said, "Bikram? As though your son was a prince! Do you know the prince's great grandfather's name was Bikram and you dare to call your child by such an aristocratic name!"

Jhankuli trembled in fear instantly. She spat on herself too. Right, how could her son's name be similar to that of the grandpa of the prince? At last she called him "Makar". During kingship, labourers and subjects dared not call their children with decent names, such as Saurav, Gaurab, Ranjan, etc. Instead they called them Suria, Raia, Baya, Pacha, Hagura, etc. Similarly they used to call their daughters Pachi, Mandi, Gurubari, Mangili, etc. instead of Puspa, Adya, Nandita, Bandana,etc. – very decent names indeed. She was obliged to God after giving her son such a name, Makar. Makar twice complained to her, "Mother, people are slandering us as leftovers eaters. So, let us not take any leftovers anymore." But Jhankuli had no courage to desist from the habit. And now only she felt courageous as the fat man gave an alternative. A mother could do anything for her children.

Next evening she waited for that gentleman at the fixed place. He arrived there within ten minutes and asked her –"What did you decide? Would you work in a hotel?" Jhankuli said–"Yes".

-You will be paid fifteen hundred rupees per month and a meal you could take home daily in gratis too. Wait for me here next morning. I shall take you to the hotel. You will start working there from tomorrow.

-Yes, she said. The man departed on the bike swiftly like a leaf in a storm. One thousand five hundred rupees! She felt like reeling. Now her hand would hold so many wads of notes, the hand that had never touched even one hundred! Could she keep herself normal? Suddenly her right hand started shaking. She clasped it with her left hand.

-Mother, what happened to your hand? Asked Makar. Jhankuli was nonplussed how to express that her hand turned powerless even before holding fifteen hundred rupees which she had even never dreamt of. No, she must strengthen her hand.

Jhankuli had not a wink of sleep that night. She felt more embarrassed about bidding good bye suddenly to the work which got her leftovers than accepting employment in the hotel. She also felt obsessed with a feeling as if she had lost the power of smelling. How sweet are the vagaries of mind! The mind that was bent upon leaving the heinous habit of eating leftovers, now loved it because of habit. She felt immeasurably exultant about working in a hotel as she thought of her children. She drew her sleeping children towards her and wrapped them in her hand as if to save them from the spear of eating leftovers. She felt as though these children were in her uterus still and she would give them a new birth!

Leaving her children at home she presented herself in front of the hotel as bidden by that fat man. She was amazed to cast a glance at the hotel. She forgot her physical presence as she looked at its five-story building. Coming to her senses she felt as though the wind blowing in front of the hotel cautioned her – "Go away, go!" She considered herself quite diffident to stand there, not to speak of entering it by the front door. But the next moment she got puffed up with pride that she was one of its employees. Now she could retort her neighbourers and Buddhi too that she was no more working in exchange for getting leftovers. She was an employee of the Rangaranga Hotel, getting monthly emolument. Yes, she would gravely spell out "Rangaranga Hotel."

Jhankuli entered the hotel through its back door, squatted squeamishly at a dirty place full of broken bricks, empty gas cylinders, pieces of torn cloth, broom, etc. A male and two female employees came out from the washing room. They were clad in green.

The leader, an old man asked, "Are you Jhankuli? Will you work here?"

Jhankuli nodded her head in agreement. She got acquainted with them and came to know that several social ceremonies such as marriage, sacred thread, birth day were arranged there. So also feasts for them. Besides, usual cooking was done in the hotel.

The leader gave her a green sari which she put on and got engaged in washing utensils and other cooking accessories. The leader instructed her everything. A marriage was solemnised next day. The feast was over. Jhankuli was greatly astounded as she saw a huge amount of leftovers. She sat in terrible shock, stared at the sky. The moon was getting blackened, the wind slowing down. The sensitising flavour of the leftovers thrown there scourged her viciously to bleed. She burst into tears. She felt every feast at every hotel wasted so much, heaps after heaps, while lakhs of innocent starving visages got buried under such waste.

- What happened? Why are you crying? The leader asked.

- Let all the starving people of the country be given the leftovers............No, no! She paused.

■

The Pond Heron

Climate changes in winter every three hours-cold, then soothing warm morning, followed by scorching sunshine, then amiable sun, mild cold and biting cold. One experiences these even in a single day. People too change their apparel accordingly. The pond heron, sitting on the edge of the river, pondered about the wayfarers wending their way along the road in front of it. It was there for a long time in quest of food but to no purpose. It sat on the patch of sand beside the shrunk stream of the river that flowed serpentine. The stream was shrunk and transparent to show even when a fish swam in it. The heron felt extremely exhausted waiting for weary hours, completely shaken mentally. It darted its look towards the oxen grazing under a dried date tree.-"O, how contented they look! How hilariously the farmers hum tunes from and to paddy fields. But only I wait and wait beside the river just to fill my belly; O God, why did you make me carnivorous? Or else I would be flying merrily like pigeons, crows relishing paddy, cucumber, fruits, etc!" It heaved a deep sigh with all such monologues.Green leaves of garlic plant in the paddy field that touched its feet were gorgeously swaying upward. The heron contemplated to taste it a bit. As it bit a leaf, it contorted itself because of its pungent smell . It felt like vomiting, producing "ah...ah" sound. The oxen grazing under the date tree and the passersby looked at it. Even some other herons sitting near the river stared at the heron. They thought, might be the heron had gulped down a big fish whose bones had jammed its throat! Well taught!

The heron could guess their sneer from their demeanour and froze in shame. – O, God ! how silly to be troubled so much simply by tasting such a leaf! Why did you make me carnivorous? What an irony! A bird flying in the sky haunts for its food in water! Hell with my being a bird."

The crane shrank with such thoughts, but its beak turned more sharpened. A small crab emerged from a small hole on the loose earth on which the heron sat. It's feathers and tail trembled. Its eyes glistened. It spelt out 'ah' in exclamation. It looked at the crab intently and murmured, "I remember, your grandpa or maybe its grandpa or its grandpa had stifled my grandpa or his grandpa's neck to death because it was greedier for crab's flesh than that of fish. It, indeed, was traitorous, selfish and ungrateful towards its friend. But I won't be greedy for that and get throttled to death by you."

Soliloquizing this, it marked each movement of the crab and thought it wise to move away from that place in quest of food rather than stay there in a state of fear. As it stepped forward a little, the crab said to it, "Hello, dear pond heron, why do you flee away? Well, I come close to you just to have some chit chat but you run away! Strange!"

Such fascinating words made the heron's eyes sparkle. Yet in a tone of despondence, it said, "No, my friend; I have remained starved throughout the day as I failed to get even a grig. Hence I decide to move elsewhere in search of food."

-You see, the river water is poisoned as pesticides sprinkled on paddy fields and chemicals of factories have mixed with it. How can grigs live in such water? And you feel avid for getting grigs! Look, every year lakhs of birds migrate from thousands of miles to Chilika, but you stupid, good for nothing, you are searching grigs in river!

The crab's words brought lustre to the crane's eyes. How come, a crab living inside a hole could collect news of the world! It wondered. It must have kept contact with the entire animal kingdom. The heron appreciated the crab mentally but thought it better to keep body and soul together somehow in its own native place rather than flying elsewhere. Everything there was marvellous and very much akin –the river, that tree, that field, the sunset and residents, it thought.

-Listen my friend! The river water, after some days, will turn so dangerous that if you dip your legs in it, these will get destroyed. Haven't you seen how big gudgeons and sheat- fish have got wounded? Hence it is wise to act according to the demands of circumstances- the crab told in an explanatory manner which the crane took to its heart. It felt the truth of the crab's words.

In a voice of melancholy it asked," Well, I may fly to another place, but what about you?"

-Yes, I am also worried about that – what shall I do? With this expression the crab marked the signs on the crane's face.

The crane turned straight, attentive, and imagined the power that the crab's legs had. Could these legs throttle me? It might do so. Suspecting that I would swallow it taking it to a tree while flying in the sky after befriending it.

The heron's suspicion thickened. It thought it would be irrational to assume that the crab's legs were feeble because these looked thin. It heaved a deep breath.

The crane turned thoughtful about how an accident that had happened generations ago had been able to erect a wall of suspicion for hundreds of years. It reprimanded its forefather who was the accomplice; who had befriended the crab, betrayed it and was consequently killed by it.

Now the pond heron widened its eyes optimistically. Well, this was a golden opportunity to amend; it could dispel that darkness of suspicion, and open a new chapter of friendship and release both the creatures from that cruel tale of the crab and the crane.

The heron expressed," Brother, I shall take you to a river free from poison."

Such proposal of the crane startled the crab; it stared at the heron but found no trace of hypocrisy on its face.

The crane asked, "Do you agree with me?" Then he said, "Look, it's late afternoon. It's time for us to go away."So saying the heron flapped its wings twice which indicated that it was excitedly ready.

The crab too felt excited and thought, it's better to flee this river to save one's skin. Such an instantaneous thought gripped it. The crab looked around and saw a few grey cranes flapping their wings. The sun was about to set. Now they would search one river after another to ascertain which of them was not contaminated. Then there would be dusk and darkness everywhere. And the crane would take it to the hollow of a tree. In pitch darkness the crane would put an end to its life; the old story of betrayal suddenly came to his mind.

The crab intended to do away with the suspicion that was beginning to engulf them. And said, "Friend, it's late today. You rather fly tomorrow to ascertain which river would be poison free. Then you will take me on your wings, we will stay together. Agree?"

-Absolutely, said the crane producing merry notes of quack.

-Why so glad? Asked the crab.

-Because you addressed me as friend.

The herons and birds flapping nearby were taken aback about the crane's delight. They looked at it and thought if it got delicious provisions at the twilight. No, were it the case, the crane could fly to a tree with it. But it stayed put there.

As the crane heaved a deep sigh, the crab asked,"What happened, pal?"

The former kept mum; it sported a melancholic smile and stooped its face.

-O, I see. You appear dejected since you failed to find out any provisions till now - the crab said in a mild voice.

-Let me go elsewhere in search of food - said the crane.

The crab nodded its head in agreement and the crane flapped its wings upward over the river in hope of some edibles. The crab marked its flight and wished him good. Then it began sauntering into its hole regretting that as an aquatic animal it failed to assist its friend in finding some provisions.

It waited a bit and raised itself on the river bank with its tiny legs and looked afar, but the crane was visible no more.

The sun was crimson. The crab spoke to itself –Had I tried, my friend could have got some provisions. I could have deceived some grigs and minnows in course of my talk with them to bring them up. And the crane could have preyed on them.

Then the crab, all at once, chided itself time and again for such an obnoxious thought, its eyes becoming almost motionless. It cursed itself – how could it harbour such a demoniac thought! Ah, doing this, it would have turned traitor. How filthy and despicable!

It entered its hole then.

For many forenoons and afternoons, the crab came out of its hole, searched the crane to no purpose. It was found nowhere. The crab loitered on the banks of the river for a while. How could my friend forget my assurance born of intimacy?

After so many days. It was 12'o clock in the day; the crab got huddled in slumber in its own hole. Repeated sounds of 'quack' broke its slumber- O' it was its friend's voice. The crab rushed out of its hole; its joys knew no bounds the moment it saw the heron. The latter too responded gleefully. The crab scrutinised the crane from its top to toe and said, "O, you look so fatigued! Where were you so long? I was waiting for you every moment." Full of enthusiasm and emotion, the crab asked "Have you got anything to eat ?"

-O, yes. I have strained much during the days gone by and have decided at last that we should move to a jungle area in the Mahanadi. Far from human habitation, the place is full of trees, and birds too. Here the current of the river is sharp and deep. The water is very transparent, a play ground of fish and crabs. No factories there. Hence water not polluted. Well, we should move there.

The crane was eager, not because it wanted to move to that place as the river there was safe and had enough food to offer, but that by going there it could efface the age old blot on the species of the crane.

So it said to the crab, "Let's hurry. It's two or three days' flight and emergencies too may occur."

The crab, though felt charmed by the crane's enthusiasm and emotionality, replied like a foreteller, "But my friend, now the more a place is solitary, the more dangerous it is. The river of that place you have seen may be clean, but that may have also been frequented by bird-catchers because of solitude. Perhaps, you have got no time to guess all this."

The crane turned still and thought, the crab may not be wrong. In fact, it was heedless about it. All at once it said, "Should we then stay here?"

The crab thought for a while and said, "No, we will move there since this place is no more conducive to us. You see, only a handful of cranes, grey cranes are loitering here like last emblems. Let's then start for the new place.'

An overwhelmed crane cast a glance around and thought of its long association with the area. Now it was leaving the place once and for all. It dipped its beak into the river. The crab moved round the place, looked at the sky; the sun was scorching. The crab closed its hole with its tiny legs and said to the crane, "Dear friend, now I am ready."

The crane flapped its wings; gathered its strength and held the crab in its beak. The two felt a sharp biting sensation with their first touch. Very much excited they became intimate with a deep sense of comradeship.

With the crab in its beak, the crane took off. Birds in the river and on trees turned pale as they witnessed such a scene in the sky. People in countryside, town, animals and the plant kingdom were quite mesmerised by the scene. Some apprehended, the old story of the heron and the crab would be repeated.

Excited and ebullient, the crane darted along the sky, determined to wipe out the prolonged blot on its species. It was filled with the prowess of hundred lions, as it were. Even though it could not open its beaks , it spoke to the world vociferously, - "Look, look with your wide open eyes ; here I am girding up my loins to erase the blot that my species are traitors."

The crab, embracing the blue sky, floating clouds, rippling greenery of trees and hills, felt fortunate. Because who else other than the bird was fortunate to experience the three worlds, heaven, earth, and water? The bird alone could exert its existence in these domains.

So it said to the crane, "Indeed, you are great! I am beholden to you once and for all. But for you I won't have got such ecstatic experience. The latter said nothing because it was aware that the crab would fall to abysmal depth the moment it opened its beaks. So it flapped its wings in a different manner. The crab understood its implication. As a matter of fact, the crane's silence was for its good.

The birds flying nearby stared at them. The crane was flying. A faith was flying, valour was flying. The sun was about to set. The entire area was going to be enveloped with darkness. The crane thought, they would lose path in pitch darkness if it moved further leaving such a known place. Hence it perched in the hollow of a banyan tree on the edge of a tank. It let the crab off its beaks and said, "My dear, let's spend the night here. We'll start the journey next morning."

The crab was already beside itself with joy as it had seen so many areas, dreamlands, almost excellent pageantry of beauty. Indeed, the crane was a friend like friend. It described before the crane its inward ecstasy at the time of flying, hanging from the crane's beak. The crane smiled a little and said, 'This is my old place. The tank beside the tree was our shelter but got poisoned as a man in conflict with the owner of the tank sprinkled poison in it. Consequently all aquatic creatures residing in it died and we too left the place. Well, let us see if the water is still poisoned or otherwise. If it is poisonous no more, I shall fetch a lump of mud for you. Will you relish it?

-No, I need nothing. Better you find something for yourself. You laboured a lot.

The crane flew from the edge of the tank. Casting its glance all around searchingly, the crab entered the hollow of the tree. The pitch darkness inside the hollow trembled it. To its consternation it discovered there fish bones galore. But it consoled itself within no time and thought it natural since the crane used to stay here, it must have preyed on a lot of fish and eaten those there. Hence it need not worry. The crab breathed heavily and came out of the hollow. At dusk, when the crane returned, the crab asked the former if it had got anything to eat.

-"No, though the tank water is so transparent now."It replied.

Then it sat on a branch silently. Its silence revived in the crab its old suspicion about the scattered fish bones in the hollow. The crab looked at the crane with a pinch of suspicion. It could no more take the crane as its friend. The crane appeared to be a predator which might kill it anytime to satiate its hunger. The crab too became cautious. The night grew as much dangerous as the silence between them. At times, the crane's eyes turned greedy. It looked at the crab but chided itself – "Fie on you, be silent, O, greedy self ! You may die from hunger but don't look at the crab greedily. Be cautious, you are up to wiping out the blot on your species."

While the crane had not a wink of sleep due to hunger, the crab too suffered from insomnia owing to its suspicion against the crane. To get rid of such mental tension the crane said: Dear friend, tell me a tale so that my hunger will vanish.

The night was getting dense, darkness being pitch among leaves and branches of trees. The crab spoke to itself – Well , not story but food is essential for satisfying hunger. And I am your desired object at this moment. Soon it shed such tantalizing thought soliloquising –How can you think so badly of your friend who has its every nerve to serve you? It would have devoured you on any tree on the way had it desired so.

The crab erased all such evil thoughts and said, "My dear, why a story, I shall tell you a piece of truth. Listen. The hollow of this tree is filled with fish bones. Haven't you eaten fish?"

The crane felt embarrassed and convulsed with these words so much so that it dashed its beak against a branch of the tree. What a blunder he made by selecting such a resting place for their shelter! The age-old story of how the crab had squeezed the crane's throat just after it had seen the fish bones came to his mind. Was its friend, turning suspicious about it? It became very thoughtful. In darkness neither could mark the emotion their faces played. In an intense state of friendship, with a view to expiating, the crane had forgotten any possibility of arousing an atmosphere of suspicion in the event of taking shelter in the hollow of a tree. It said sadly, 'My friend, that had happened long long ago. I was oblivious of it. But are you worried about it?"

The crab thought- O, I was altogether unnerved the moment I saw it." However it spoke without any fear- No room for any worry ? But is it not important to maintain friendship?

The crane felt immeasurably inspired by such words. It got thrilled as it visualised that the crane of that old story feeling guilty for all time to come. It spoke to the latter mentally- Now you can sit upright and wait.

The night was deep and dark. Water in the tank looked dark now. Trees around were mute in deep sleep. At times silence was broken due to sounds made by squirrels, and small insects in the trees.

Being famished, the crane was dozing in the joint of branches. Though the crab felt sleepy, it remained awake as a hungry crane might be a danger.

It dawned. Everything became visible. The crab, completely sleepless throughout the night, twinkled its eyes. The last night was quite ghastly and unforgettable. Now it was cheerful. It could locate the crane sleeping in its front. Hunger and flight throughout the day had fatigued it so much as to sleep so sound. Now the chirping of birds on the nearby tree was heard. The crab repented for its suspicion against the crane throughout the night. But, it might also be that as it remained awake in the entire night, the crane dared not attack it. Brushing all these thoughts aside, the crab came near the crane and caressed its feet. The latter woke up and smiled as it saw the crab nearby. The entire tree shivered with its typical quack, quack sound.

-Enjoyed a sound sleep? Asked the crab.

-O, yes- replied the crane and looked at it attentively. Surprisingly it asked the crab, "You seem to have no sound sleep. Is it?

- "Don't you know the crab is no bird so that it can sleep on a tree? It lives in water and on earth." The crane nodded its head in agreement.

-Let me go now in search of some food. I shall fetch you a lump of mud on my way back. Then we would fly and try to reach the Mahanadi before evening.

The crane flapped its wings in the sky while the crab enjoyed the silvery dawn. The sky, earth, trees, tank were getting exposed by degrees, colour descending everywhere.

The crab looked for the crane but found it nowhere. When its eyes swam into the hollow of the tree, it felt the rise of the past story of the crane and the crab in its innermost heart. In fact, suspicion engulfs all, whosoever they are. Moment after moment passed in frenzy.

The crab became normal as it heard the sound of the crane's wings. The former placed a lump of mud that it had carried in its beak and sat silent. The crab gulped down some amount of it and asked-"Did you get anything to eat?

-O, yes, I have drunk water to fill my belly. Saying so, the crane heaved a deep breath and continued "I'll fetch something from the Mahanadi. Finish your meal. We will start."

The crab turned frigid. It got confused whether it should journey elsewhere with the help of someone who was hungry. The crane could very well mark the crab's worry and anxiety and said, "Don't feel troubled, my friend. A bird like me can fly to three worlds –sky, earth, water. Also it can fly to distant places even without food. Let's start now."

The crane prepared itself how to reach that jungle area in the Mahanadi. There it would alight the crab and finally rescue its own species from a prolonged ignominy.

The crab finished taking mud. Both smiled to their heart's content. The crane held the crab in its beak and flapped its wings in the sky cautiously on its way to that jungle area of the Mahanadi. It thought it was carrying in its beak the past, present and future of its species. The crane flew rapidly darting along the sky with vim, vigour and valour. The sun was scorching. The crane covered miles crossing mountains and hills, with the crab in its beak. After a while it felt its belly burning in fire. It had been starved for the last two days. Only air and water was its food. Such an arduous flight! Sweet smell flowed into its mouth. Saliva streamed from its throat. The crane trembled. As a result, its wings zigzagged. Bewildered, it felt such sweet smell, such saliva to be the instinctive relationship between the consumer and food.

The crane remained unwavering, consoled its subconscious- No, don't be so rash, you devil! It is the saviour of our species which I carry in my beak. I have taken a vow to rescue our species from a curse with its help. Please be not greedy about the relationship of the eater and food.

The crane determined. But it felt the fire of hunger in belly while it carried food in its beak. It tried every nerve to restrain itself from such devastating thought and accelerated the pace of its flight just to desist itself from the fiery furnace of hunger. It could forget its hunger as it became conscious and cautious that excessive speed spells disaster. But how long could it resist the 'natural' in it? Saliva streamed down from its beak. The grip of its beak started to squeeze the crab. Yet the crane determined not to consume the crab, its friend and saviour. Its hunger grew intolerable; saliva flowed nonstop. Tears rolled down the eyes of a committed crane, flying fiercely towards the river, praying to all "O, give me strength in such a crisis so that I can restrain myself." It flew and flew.

The crab, feeling the crane's hunger from the latter's grabbing of its throat, felt nonplussed; the hoary past danced before it- Once upon a time, in the pretext of friendship, the crane had tried to swallow the crab, consequent upon which the crab had throttled the crane's neck. The species of the crane still carried that stigma. The crab never suspected the friendship. But, now the prey is in the mouth of the hungry. The crab felt the warm stream of saliva flowing from the crane's mouth. Out of sheer eagerness to gulp down the food, saliva runs from its beak to throat, thought the crab. It turned more perplexed.

The crane looked onward. Their destination was not far off. It determined to cover the distance, overcome the excruciating hunger. Let all saliva flow but it won't let the beak to be wild. Hence, it accelerated its speed while a lump of saliva streamed from its throat once again. Suddenly it felt a sharp stinging leg piercing its head fiercely. The crab collecting all might in its one leg, attacked the crane's beak like a spear, the only unfailing weapon to protect itself.

The wounded crane remained quiet though its muscles were irresistible to cry. Streams of blood oozing from its beak were dripping on leaves of trees. It soliloquized- "Friend, how can you know that saliva flows only when food is in the consumer's mouth, yet it does not swallow that food ? It restrains itself against this."

The crane didn't open its mouth knowing full well that the crab would fall the moment it opened its mouth. So it would be its defeat.

-Don't deceive anymore, crane! You will fall down dead in no time. You reaped the consequences of betraying a friend. Your species are like that –said the crab.

Still blood streaming down from its beak, the crane flew onward swifter and carefree. It felt parched in its throat, its physical strength waned and life force dimmed. As it approached the solitary sylvan setting in the Mahanadi, it beamed with joy. But, for a while. The sun had slightly slanted towards west from the mid sky. It alighted on the river bank, blood dripping and tears trickling. As soon as it set its feet on sand near water it opened the grip of its beak and fell flat. The crab got out loosening its leg already thrust into the crane's throat. The stream flowed into the

Mahanadi. Faintly the bird said, "My friend, this is the river, our destination. You wounded me out of suspicion. I could have thrashed you dead against a tree but after all I am your friend."

The crab got startled, held the crane's legs apologetically. It caressed the latter's face and said, "My friend, it is difficult to comprehend one thing in the world. It is saliva."

By that time the eyeballs of the bird had paled.

: "You finished the story of thousand years in a moment. You, my real friend!" The crab's emotion - chocked feeble voice got melted in the murmurs of the Mahanadi.

Darkness Impenetrable

C hema's mother was in tears. Tears-hot and wild dropped on earth. She cried while winnowing paddy with a winnowing fan (Kula) made of bamboo. Halting her work at times she cried so inconsolably that it created a rhythm of cry. Passersby, especially peasants carrying hay stacks on their shoulders, driving stack-ridden oxen would look at her with emotion. Her cry appeared to be a flood of time, as it were. For this she would fall unconscious at times. People would gather around her and sprinkle water on her face to regain her consciousness. She was the first person to start winnowing paddy fallen on earth and mixed with dust. At the harvesting time the extremely old women of this democratic country are compelled to be on roads with walking stick, basket and kula in biting cold on winter mornings when labourers carry hay stacks on their shoulders or by oxen. Of course, the democracy that allows life to slide with the destiny of individuals helps turn the last days of these old women into sovereign paupers. Chema's mother was crying because she had to sit along the way that ran by her own farm land. The field was hers last year; it belonged to Natia Mohanty this year. Suddenly she burst in anger, 'You bloody brat, why cutting ear of corn from the hay stacks of my land? So unscrupulous !" Baina, one of the mischievous brats doing this rushed to her and taunted-

"This old hag is very rough. Hello, is this your land, so you shout so loudly? Look, I shall also barb you with harsh words." He left seething with fury and busying himself cutting ears of corn. Chema's mother just continued staring and the Kula in her hand remained immobile. An intense spate of darkness surrounded her.

-She sold this land last year. So, why sulking over it as if it was still hers! Ownership of the land had changed. True. Yet attachment, affiliation to it was not yet over. Yes, she committed a blunder still thinking the piece of land belonged to her.

Two years back while she started to go for collecting corn scattered on road at the harvesting season, her son snatched away the basket from her hand and said-"Well, mother, have you seen any one eking out his living just by begging? You have been doing this work since my childhood. But now I don't like this." She obeyed as bidden by her son. But now no more was she able to collect paddy kneeling down. Hence she took recourse to winnowing dust mixed paddy fallen along road. Chema's mother often heard hooting of the owl. She sighed and began separating large pebbles from the collected corn.

Suji approached her with long strides hanging a gunny bag, broom, etc and pressing a betel leaf in her mouth. All at once she snatched the winning kula from Chema's mother and did the work. "See, it's afternoon, damn, you have only winnowed this small amount of corn since morning! Now, let's go home." Suji said.

Suji was adamant, out spoken. She was both the daughter and daughter-in law of this village. One after another four persons she married, but none remained with her. She drove them away with her masculinity. None would match her, she complained. She has been grazing amatorially herself outside for the last three years. She was earning too. Amazonian, she could overthrow a couple of robust males. She has been blessed with a son, illegitimate. Who knew whose seed's fruit he was!" If anyone jeered at her, she would retort instantly, "Is there any virulent male in our village to challenge me, let him come, I will see!"This way she would ridicule. However, she was very industrious. While separating small pebbles from the corn collected by Chema's mother and depositing it in her basket, she commented –"Lo, before the crow crows in the dawn, you came here and yet you couldn't collect half a basket of paddy! What sort of winnowing!"

Chema's mother got puzzled. She felt astonished finding others collecting so much corn, though she came earlier than them and would return after them. She never felt fatigued nor did she stop winnowing. She failed to fathom the mystery. A ripple of surprise crossed her mind leaving her with a world of wild thoughts. Nonplussed, she asked Suji. Suji burst into a peal of laughter and said, "You are newly yoked. First, you harness yourself to a mode of threshing .You will know how much labour it entails. Look my dear, every piece of work has its mechanism. Even begging too. You must know that. Otherwise you will return empty-handed .Similarly, you may go on brooming road but how can you get grains of paddy if it has not fallen there? That's why the easiest means is to sit where corn adequately falls off haystack. In fact, at bridges, slopes and elevations, grains of corn get shaken more, hence fall more. One who knows this sits there. understand ?"

Chema's mother was taken aback. Lo, it was so mysterious! She never thought of this.

-Well, let us go now; it is too late. Suji said.

Gathering her winnowing fan and basket, Chema's

mother stood up. Her eyes turned towards the land that once belonged to her. Baina, in some children's company was still busy cutting ear of corn. She was about to speak but shut her lips. A drop of tear, hot indeed, trickled down her cheeks. She held her staff and paced homeward straightway.

It was desolate when she opened her gate of wattles. She halted for a while; had no desire to enter home. She cast a glance at her hut from the gate, heaved a deep sigh. Chema had started building a mud house near her hut; only three layers of its wall had been raised. That was almost damaged. Chema had also sowed seeds of some vegetables. It had sprouted. Then the end… "My Chema…my son…!" With a gush of emotion for her son, she crouched herself with a thud on the verandah. Grains of corn she had collected in her basket got scattered all around. The scene of her son sprinkling water on vegetable leaf seedlings appeared before her and she kept mum for a while.

-Bloody fools! you rascals! Why don't you die from snake-bite? Why doesn't thunderbolt strike you? Curse on you rouges, die prematurely. What have you done, you bastards, you tortured my son. Damn, reborn as dogs!"- Hurling a volley of abuses she fell down there on the verandah and remained so till the evening. A neighbouring girl, Gouri approached her and said, "Dear, rise now, it's evening!"

-What do you say? Evening! Chema's mother wondered.

-Yes.

-It's all dark, my girl! So saying, she went on beating her head on the ground, wailing.

Chema's mother told, " My son, now you are grown-up. Tell me how we can live with the yield from half an acre of land? Besides, we suffer from flood this year and drought next year. Do one thing. When the Choudhury family of this village was zamidar, your father worked for them from his twelfth year till death. The dead old Choudhury's son is a number one contractor at Bhubaneswar. He lives in a palatial building. Meet him straight and tell him that I have sent you. I am sure, he will appoint you."

Obeying mother, Chema came to meet contractor Choudhury at Bhubaneswar. He was stunned to see his sky kissing building and read 'Be aware of the Dog' written on the gate. His mere elementary education at the village did not make him wise to understand such caution. Why be aware of the dog ! He wondered and stood still for a moment and remembered that he kicked so many dogs in his village to set them right. What more could this dog be? Thus he thought and entered the gate paying least heed to the warning. He was quite defiant. No sooner had he entered the gate, than the dog barked incessantly and rushed towards him.

A black dog, full of fur that hung downward, had the body of a bear. Its eyes were burning. It was violent enough to exert its long-suppressed liberty, as it were. It was prepared to bite someone as per its desire. Chema was frightened. The clothes he put on were about to be wet. In fact, the dog was so violent; otherwise such warning wouldn't be there on the gate. The dog was rushing towards Chema. Suddenly a woman's voice uttered, "Hello! Papu, Papu!" Immediately the dog's eyes turned sober; it turned towards its mistress. A dazed Chema too paced onward drooping his head. As if he was being drawn to gallows ! The maiden in his front threw a chop of meat towards her right side field. Papu ran towards it. She asked Chema haughtily, "Who do you want?" Her discourteous address hurt Chema beyond measure. He felt exasperated though he controlled himself as he had been there for a piece of job.

-Is Sir there? I have come from the village. He said.

-What Sir? Here everyone is sir. Even our servants and cooks are addressed as Sirs. Which sir do you need? - She said.

-Our Choudhury sir, contractor. I belong to his village. Mother has sent me to him for a job.

The damsel got irritated and said, "How dare you address him as Choudhury Contractor! Are you his equal? You uncouth, barbarian! He is sir of sirs, understand?"

How could Chema know about such courtesy? What mistake in addressing choudhury sir, Contractor sir! He failed to understand. The girl's apparel hanging tight to her heels was strange to him. It exposed her bulging breasts, hips and thighs.

-Will you serve here? She asked.

-My father spent his entire life serving your family when you had zamindari at our village. He is no more. We are very poor. I have come here as my mother bade me. I can do household work. Will sir employ me?

The girl remained silent and threw another chop of meat strongly to her left hand side. Papu thought it to be his and ran towards it. But it stopped as the girl called it fondly "Come here" and the dog returned to her with hungry eyes.

-Run, yes, run as fast as you can and bring the chop of meat, she commanded Chema.

- What, he would collect the chop of meat for the dog! Should he run for that for which the dog ran? Was he the dog's contestant? He felt extremely downcast but what could he do? After all, he was there for a job. Maybe, it was a test for him. Hence he ran, ran very fast with might and main. He had never run so fast in his life. As he was about to reach the chop of meat, the maiden ordered him to stand there. Chema obeyed. Then he ran back at her command. He felt he became her minion, could not touch that chop of meat. Now he would do as bidden by somebody else's whim. Where's his own will?

The girl called Papu and pointed her finger at the meat chop. Then the dog ran to its dear food item. Chema stood as before. He thought to sit down there for rest. But couldn't. He felt everything there-his sitting, his standing, his talking-couldn't be done as per his wish. His life would run by some other's order. Just then one ultra-modern car entered. A tall robust person alighted. Addressing him as Daddy, the girl ran to him and took the cigar from his lips and smoked. Chema was amazed; he couldn't know he was his master Mr Choudhury. In fact, he was unfamiliar with the girl's address "Daddy". As Mr. Choudhury rolled his eyes surprisingly on Chema who stood at a short distance the girl said, "I have chosen him as my personal servant. His interview too is over."

-Well, as you like, Leera. Then he indicated Chema to come near. But Chema couldn't go very near him. As if someone obstructed! An immediate thought that he was his master engulfed his mind. He prostrated before him. The master didn't ask him to get up. But he rose and narrated in detail the story of his coming from his village to that town. His narration didn't affect Mr. Choudhury any way, he marked.

-I don't like my servant speaking so much. He expressed gravely and went inside home in long strides, cigar in mouth.

Chema remembered his mother's aphorism, "Either be a king or be near him." But he was now able to understand its connotation. How terrible it was to be very close to King!

-Your past identity is meaningless here. You are no more Chema, you are Sapu henceforth. My personal servant, understand! Leera said to Chema.

Chema was not surprised but felt excruciatingly tortured for loss of his identity as man. As Leera had named him Sapu rhyming with her dog's name Papu, he thought –"I am no other than a dog !" His anger grew at Papu as if it was his only rival there!

Now Chema couldn't talk or smile as per his will. He had lost the spontaneity of facial expression of his feelings. He had learnt to wait standing at some distance from his mistress. His hands had turned so mechanical that his feeling of showing respect to someone would come only after saluting him. He was forgetting the usages of words and language and losing power to translate his thought into language. Even when he had no scope to speak how could language be at his command! If asked to narrate the autobiography of a dog, he won't be able to deliver even if all about its life rolled before him like a pageant. The language of slavery is weak. Gradually the language of human is getting weaker, it seems. As if, man is getting transformed into an obedient dog by degrees! Now Sapu got infuriated the moment he saw Papu. Yet, he couldn't express. How could man turn inanimate if he could translate his thought into language? Even if Papu did something or bark without rhyme and reason it was forgiven as an animal. But he was not that fortunate. He was never let off by his mistress for any irregularity.

In the solitariness of night Sapu would become

Chema. Layers of transformation would fall off his body. Then he would perceive the difference between Chema and Sapu. He would be surprised. The thoughts rising in his mind would spread on his face that turned unusual. He would feel overwhelmed. In frenzy he would desire fervently to be Chema for all time. He would want to kick off his job. But where would he go? What would he do in his village? How could he get rid of the torment of becoming a dog day by day? Chema felt utterly helpless. At dawn he felt he had turned into Sapu again-Papu's contestant. When he mets Papu alone he became Chema. His visage would became red. He cast an unusually irritating glance at it. Papu too would bark in reaction. As Chema assumed Sapu, it flung its tail and went away without remonstrance. Chema had tried time and again to be away from such competition but in vain. He had been made the rival of a dog and the competition was nonstop.

It was twilight. Sapu found Leera not in her room. He searched every other room but to no purpose. He had no routine work now; he felt relaxed and entered the garden in a happy state. Often he went there to pacify his mind even though for a moment. He would gaze at flowers, get lost in soliloquies – 'O my dear flowers, you too are becoming dog. You will grow as your master likes you to grow. You will be decorated as your master wishes. Yet he thought, the master couldn't control the smile of the flower and its sway in the wind. Was he not comparable to flowers? Was he inferior to them? As a matter of fact, he walked to the garden to dream of his freedom just looking at the innocent smile and sway of flowers.

But what came to his view now ! He got flabbergasted. Horrible! Leera lay naked with an unknown young person. He was also stark naked. They were in close clasp. Chema turned back, though, he felt excited as if warm air touched him. He wanted to enjoy the scene again but couldn't. Immediately he was transformed into Sapu. Thus he was about to retreat silently but halted by Leera's call. By that time Leera and the anonymous young man had put on their clothes.

-You came to the garden just for a stroll, isn't it? She asked.

A speechless Sapu hung his head down. "Who is he?" the young man asked.

- Sapu. She replied.

- What?

- Yes, Ashok, one is Papu and the other Sapu. But the difference is Papu would have barked at you while Sapu couldn't do that.

Smiling, they left, tormenting Sapu in mentally: "Is he inferior to the dog?" Papu has freedom to bark which he doesn't have! He is so lowly for Leera that she cared him a fig even though he saw her romancing with a young man ! Even she didn't say-' Sapu, well, you haven't seen anything, isn't it? Is he so trifling? "His blood curdled fiercely. Was this a century waiting for untrammelled sexuality?"

Chema stood on the grassy patch of the garden where Leera had exposed her nude body. His eyes reddened. Cupid's arrows pierced every fibre of his body. From Sapu he became Chema. Flowers in the garden became unpretentiously faithful before him. In an overwhelming state of excitement he started rolling on the soft bed of grass where Leera had slept.

Henceforth Sapu would become Chema again and again. His head hung down when he saw Leera in his front. He was nervous enough to look at her straight. But he looked at her intently when she was not in his front. Whenever he saw her, he perceived her still nude. As a result, his face would contort in hatred. Suddenly he would remember he was Sapu. Much of hatred against his mistress was unwarranted. Hence he would compulsorily bring his face to normalcy.

It was evening. Chema went to hand over the toiletries to Leera which he purchased from market. He saw her lying on bed, eyes closed. Chema thought her asleep and placed the items on her table. As he was about to leave Leera asked if he had bought all items. Chema was taken aback- What, she was not asleep! Maybe she lay out of fatigue or she was ill.

-Yes, Madam. Aren't you well? Should I call in a doctor, he said.

-No, I am too tired. Will you massage my legs?

Chema felt awkward-Ah, he would massage her legs which Papu wouldn't! Undone, he agreed. Massaged her legs and felt electrified. Instead of hatred for her he felt a close embrace clasping him. Strange, man's inner doggy becomes intimate just as one's mouth turns sweet when one devours sweet-poison.

-Oh. This light aggravates my headache, saying so Leera switched off bed light and drew Sapu to her lap. Darkness turned more impenetrable. Sapu danced in Leera's hand like a newly bought toy.

After a while Sapu came out of the dark room and found Papu standing there. The dog barked as it marked signs of irritation on Sapu's face. It looked at him sharply, still barking.

-May I be able to bark like you? May I impose my wishes? Couldn't I? Am I so impotent and inanimate? With these exciting thoughts, Sapu barked like a dog-Bho, Bho. Bho!

Papu too competed with him barking aloud.

Sapu barked: Bho, Bho...

Papu barked: Bho, Bho...

Their barking continued competitively. It became intense. Leera came out of her room and burst into laughter marking such competition between a dog and a man, assuming the traits of a dog. At last Papu was about to jump on to Sapu in anger. But as Leera called it, it restrained itself. Sapu went away with long strides. The lawn, flooded with neon light, turned into a burial ground for him. Flowers, trees, branches, grass were dogs for him. Did he become a dog to-day, and barke like it? He failed to understand how it came to pass! Yes, when in village, he had barked like a dog many a time. That was only a token of his happy, whimsical behaviour. But today he barked not out of happiness but as a contestant. Did he bark to be free? Chema felt he was losing everything by degrees.

Henceforth Leera's legs would ache every evening. So she would lie on bed and ask Sapu to massage. As Sapu would start massaging she would switch off light. And Sapu would come out of her room sweating profusely. He would try to cover up his annoyance and hatred writ large on his face. He would bark as Papu barked as if in a competition. Now he would think everyday how to get rid of such animosity. But he would fail. Hence he would get indulged in that usual routine work.

One day. Before evening, he started for market for domestic articles. Leera bade him to return within half an hour but he returned late deliberately. He was afraid as he was late. His strides were slow. He was surprised not finding Leera in the house. He went to the garden. It was desolate. Then he walked towards Leera's room stealthily. The room was dark. He stopped at the threshold. Suddenly the room was flooded with light. Sapu was aghast as he saw Leera lying on bed stark naked. He couldn't believe his eyes. Her eyes were closed, face sweating. She was content and fatigued. Papu, her dog was lying on her lap, tired altogether.

Leera opened her eyes. She got startled to find Sapu in her front. In no time she wrapped herself with a piece of cloth and kicked the dog down. A fatigued Papu left but without barking at Sapu as before.

Full of surprise and contempt, Sapu went down stairs. Indeed there was no difference between Sapu and Papu? Was Leera turning into a bitch? Doesn't human bear a dog-attitude at her cohabitation with the dog? Sapu found a black curtain spreading in his front, which, even if reflected by a white light, still looked blacker.

At dawn Papu was found dead in the garden, blood oozing forth from its neck and tongue outstretched. And Chema was absconding.

-Killing my dog is tantamount to killing mastership, transgressing authority. One who has not petted a dog can ill afford to rear a man. Shouted Choudhury.

The last scene of this story: Towards the evening Chema's mother was seen crying and shouting in a plaintive tone -You brutes, you killed my only son, the apple of my eye. Curse on you, die, and die now, reborn as dogs!

■

18 Exile Road

The Art College in front of his residence. Running in a rented house though. On its portico lie dozens of statues, finished and half-finished. Pasted on the easel, a sheet of art paper: colours, brush and a piece of cloth kept on the table nearby.

Nitish stares at it through window. At times, he jumps over the gate and looks intently at the statues and the artists engrossed in carving them. The artists turn images for him for a moment. On being conscious, he becomes quizzical, 'why such feeling?' He closes and opens his eyes. The physical contours of the artist dispel his illusions.......no, they are human beings.

Close to the street, the art college catches everyone's eye, young and old. They stroll around such a creative world casually though. The statue of a maiden, robust and rotund, on the portico was their cynosure, now shifted to a corner of the portico, wrapped completely. There stands another statue, a bird sucking the teat of a woman's breast, while a baby below looks at her bereaved. The woman's eyes are closed; she is virtually a mother. Whoever sees the statue, is transported to an empyrean beyond his physical existence. Students of the art college are never time bound, so has Nisith felt.

Period and time.....matter little for art. It may take

minutes or months to carve the eye of a statue. Nisith gets topsy-turvyed when he cogitates such supra-real matters. At times he wakes up in the dead of night, opens window and gazes at the interior of the art college.

That night, he saw in flood light an artist lost in work. The wall clock chimed 2 past 18. He sat on his bed quite bemused and enjoyed the artist's absorption. Half an hour passed. Sabujima, his wife woke up and marked her husband's ecstasy with amazement. She realised Nisith was beyond space and time. She nudged him. Nisith came down the earth and ejaculated, "Lo, art conquers slumber". But Sabujima forced him to sleep with a taunt, "So what? That is the affinity between art and the artist. Not for you, please sleep now."

-Fie, aren't we stuff of art? You and I? Don't we constitute such affinity? Nisith burst out with deep emotion.

Dumbfounded, Sabujima heaved a deep breath.

One afternoon, Nisith was returning home for lunch. While crossing from the main road to the street road he halted and found four art students engaged in portraying persons passing by and presenting them with their portraits. Nisith stayed and forgot his lunch. When he was late, his wife came along the road in search of him. When he saw her he came to senses. In long strides he reached home and stated, "O, such superb art and such excellent artists take away your hunger!" His words struck Sabujima dumb. So many passersby pass by the way. They too see the statues. She herself also sees. Strange, she hasn't seen anyone forgetting hunger for hours together for the statues. Sabujima was confounded. The art college is just like any other college, she used to think. But her thought got hamstrung as she marked Nisith's unusual demeanour.

What's his vision of the art objects? Now she thought of him deeper and deeper. She paid heed to his actions seriously.

Next morning an old beggar approached her for a handful of flattened rice. She went inside the house and returned with the food stuff prayed for. But where was the beggar? Taken aback, she turned her gaze all around. Her surprise doubled as she found the old beggar staring at the statue of a cowherd boy in front of the college. The cowherd boy was playing a flute. Sabujima looked at it for a while and turned meditative. - "How strange! The old man forgot his hunger for the statue!" Then she went into her house.

The old beggar appeared again after a little while for alms, Sabujima came out with that plate of flattened rice and said, "You fellow! Forgot hunger so long for a mere statue !"

Pat came the old man's reply, 'O Mum, that's a hunger too, it reigns over physical hunger. Such hunger has made me a beggar. Once I was a cowherd boy, playing the flute. A strange instrument indeed! It monopolises its player, though it sinks him in poverty."He completed with a deep breath.

Sabujima poured the food in the plate into the old beggar's napkin. He departed not before casting a glance at the art college. Sabujima too looked that way like a fool. She failed to fathom its mystery, her thought notwithstanding.

These strange persons can create exactly as God creates. At times they surpass Him too. With a difference, they can create also; O' God, hell with these thoughts ! One needs to get rid of such hypnotism lest one be nowhere. Art is a conundrum. Damn it. She then hung unto her domestic chores. But in leisure she would feel crazy to glance through window at some recently hewn statues. She didn't know why such desire was irresistible. Yet she tried to suppress it. She thought it to be a sort of entanglement. After all, it's an art college where students were educated. That's all. But she has been marking a radical change in Nitish ever since the art college came into being. No more he gets irritated, nor does he flare up even if his guests are not well attended to, never turns over anxious about their hospitality; he appears quite genuine and grave. These changes have satisfied her, but what about their conjugal life? Losing its warmth, getting frigid. Is Nisith disillusioned? All art, music or dance, painting or acting is earthbound with its power of enticement. But what has happened to Nisith? She was confounded with these unnerving thoughts.

The wrathful mewing of a cat disturbed the quiet in front of the college. Human eyes from all quarters got fixed at it. Nisith and Sabujima jumped over the gate and hastened to the spot. They saw a real cat quarrelling with a statue-cat made yesterday. At the denouement, the cat jumped on the statue. The statue slid. The cat stood confused. It became silent and left the place casting backward glances time and again. Even after the cat's departure, the onlookers stood there transfixed. A student of the art college took snaps of the scene. Because such a scene would not have taken place elsewhere. The student felt fortunate. By this time another student had put the statue of the cat in order.

Nisith was still sailing in an unknown world. -Hello Mr., the cats' quarrel is long over. But I see. You are still in it! Sabujima thrust her hand unto him. Nisith smiled. Sabujima felt as though he were a statue, a man no more! She felt as if she had also lost something even though she had got many rare experiences because of the art college!

That night. Nisith switched on TV and then switched it off as the night grew. He pissed. Washed his legs, mouth in the bathroom. As he switched on light in the bedroom he discovered a nude Sabujima. He covered her with a bed sheet.

He got stunned hearing someone sobbing nearby. He searched here and there but of no avail. Opened the window. Moon beams flooded all around. He saw the vivacious statue of the woman at the corner of the portico of the art college gone.

His hands on the window railings got chilled.

The Call Of Blood

Past three that day, Anshupa came out of the hostel gate in company of her room mates, Sheila and Nisha. The gatekeeper pointed her at a young man of about twentyfour, standing at a distance. Clad in a shirt sold at a throwaway price on footpath, a pair of hawai chappal, a plastic bag in hand, he presented a picture of agony, anxiety and apperhension.

Anshupa queried him, "What's the matter ?" The youngman was overwhelmed with joy as though he achieved the most precious. As he saw in his front a maiden of about nineteen, in jeans,her hair cascading and mobile in hand, the young man asked if she was Anshupa.

- O, yes, why do you enquire ? retorted Anshupa point blank.

In no time the young man prostrated before her supplicating, "Please save me, Mother."

Flabbergasted, Anshupa drew back which prompted one of her mates to remark if the fellow was mad. Anshupa had already turned vexed at the way he prostrated. She did not approve of such an elderly fellow falling at her feet.

- Why did you call me for this madcap ? She fumed at the gatekeeper.

She was just returning when the young man raised himself from the ground and said, "No, Mother, I am not mad. Please listen to me attentively. I am Chhayanidhi whose mother you were in his previous birth."

Excited, Anshupa got inside, her friends giggling and one of them remarking, "A magic show indeed !." Behind them they heard Chhayanidhi-forlorn and famished-saying pathetically, "Mother, I had been to your village, Nayanpur and met your father."

Anshupa stayed put as her companions urged her to listen to what the young man said since he referred to her father. She complied. As she drew near Chhayanidhi, the latter stood up clasping his belly with groans of excruciating pain. Eyes closed, he sat down writhing.

The three friends exclaimed, "What's the matter ?" Clasping his belly with his left hand, the youngman implored them to wait. Pain subsided a while later, he gulped down water from his plastic bottle and felt relieved. The three girls became normal.

- What happened ? they asked.

- This pain, the whole trouble lies in it. So saying he stood up tottering.

- Let us sit on the bridge. Nisha suggested

The day was waning. There was rush of vehicles along the road.

Chhayanidhi started, "Listen please, my native place is Khajuripata, seventy kilometers from Nayanpur. My mother expired just after my birth. At four I began suffering from colic. Father got me treated by so many doctors - allopath, homeopath, ayurved but to no avail. Various modern medical tests confirmed that I had no stomach ailment. A lot of medicine I swallowed but to no purpose. I passed matriculation, colic notwithstanding. Entered a college then but could not continue because of unbearable pain which triggered a feeling in me to commit suicide. Though I had no faith in black magic, father insisted to go for that. Hence we went to a village called Budhatilkiri, ten kilometers away from our village."

Anshupa and her companions were quite agog, her companions becoming curious to know about the role Anshupa had in such an affair.

- There I prostrated before a deity steadfastly. The sanctum of the deity was always crowded by a vast number of people, belonging to different social hierarchies, all converging there for divine grace granted through the medium of a divinely possessed, milkman by profession. He would come to the premises of the deity at 8 o' clock in the night and return at 10. Before his arrival the crowd of people thronging there must have lain there in devout prostration for their wish fulfilment. The divinely possessed milkman would lift the "muda" kept near by.

On some days, he won't touch or lift any of it as he won't feel divinely possessed. Father and I visited him for three days. At last he blessed us lifting the muda I had placed there devoutly and shouted, "O yes, Young man suffering from colic." Hearing this we rushed to him. He told, "Elder daughter of Moti Behera, a resident on the other side of the river Bankei was your mother in your previous birth. You will be cured if you serve her and relish the leftovevs of the food she eats.."

Chhayanidhi's expression confounded Anshupa who burst out with an excited retort, "Rubbish, this is hypocrisy."

The youngman kept mum as he found Anshupa disbelieving him. Of course, he remembered, he did not believe when the divinely - possessed person broached this before him. Till today he was not fully convinced. Yet that was his last resort. Moreover,it was quite amazing when the divinely possessesd person told that Moti Behera's house was located on the other side of the river, a village of about seventy kilometers away from that fellow's village. Hence he belived him.

Anshupa's companions consoled her saying, "Don't get excited. Let him finish, then you will reply. Of course, such incidents are rare but old people in villages have testified to such occurrences."Anshupa felt being swayed to an inconceivable situation because of her companion's enthusiasm about the matter. Maybe, the stranger's life would take a dramatic turn any moment.

She too apprehended that the stranger might paralyse her. Why should one believe him because it is impossible to discern one's previous birth? Yet she kept patient because, she knew impatience is a blind alley. She sat down on the bridge and allowed Chhayanidhi to speak.

Still very panicky, the youngman continued," Thereafter, I approached your father who dismissed me as a hypocrite, a swindler. Undone, I left him fearfully. I collected your whereabouts that you are prosecuting engineering studies in electronics here. Mother, I have come here with incalculable hope. My survival depends on your mercy." Eyes beaming with hope, Chhayanidhi appealed to Anshupa in folded hands.

"Damned, why do you address me as mother ? What do you want ? "Anshupa hit back." I shall serve you Mother, relish the leftovers of your food everyday." Chhayanidhi expressed in a plaintive tone.

Anshupa moved aside and talked to her father over phone. Then she turned red in anger and shouted, 'You bloody hypocrite, You have hit upon a new trick so that we would be gazumped. Pretending colic pain! Fie on your belief in a divinely possessed person, an ultramodern trickery. Get out. If I see you here again, you will be damned."

The guard was listening to her words; hence he rushed to the youngman with abusive words," You bloody bastard, get out or I will shoot you dead."

Clasping his belly, Chhayanidhi retreated in fear sheepishly along an open road of torment. The day grew old. A rattled Anshupa returned to her room with her friends.

"I don't think the felllow is a hypocrite" Nisha remarked. Anshupa fumed,` "Then, you are up to prove that he is my son !"

Nisha did not reply as she could gauge Anshupa's smouldering rage. They kept silent for some time. Then Sheila started, 'Let us forget it and go to the beach to ease our tension". She nudged Anshupa to a smile.

- The matter must be kept secret among us. Very confidential - Nisha cautioned.

It was almost dusk when they returned to their hostel. Seeing her father strolling outside the hostel gate, Anshupa ran to him. Her friends too paid due regards to Moti babu. Moti babu was about to express something but stopped.

-Well, uncle, please speak out though we know what you are going to say. About that young man suffering from colic. We have kept the matter a secret among us and have decided not to divulge it." Said Nisha.

- Well done, it's a trouble uncalled for. Anshupa, I rushed to you the moment I heard over your phone about the young man's arrival here. Nowadays you find tricksters galore; leave it. Are you distrubed ? Asked Moti Babu.

- No, not at all, father. But I think he is not mischievous. Besides.....

Sheila pressed her foot instantly before she could complete. Anshupa understood well. Hence she twisted her sentence and said, "Father, let us not discuss the matter any more to get more depressed. It's evening. I am all right. Please stay in our guardians' mess. Don't go."

- Look, construction of our house is going on. How can I stay ? I can catch a vehicle plying on the highway.' Then Motibabu handed over a bundle of notes to her," Your mother has sent it."

"Uncle, where is that young man's native place; town or village ?" Nisha asked.

- Khajuripata, a village. I have asked a messenger to collect information about him. He will go to the village Budhatikiri, via Khajuripata to ascertain if any such divination is pronounced there. I shall take the young man to task if he is found fudgy.

The girls saw Moti babu off at the bus stand and returned to hostel.

- Uncle has done well by not divulging the matter. Otherwise pressmen, TV channels would be needling. These chaps are always ready to report such sensational news. If they so desire, they can slap photograph of Anshupa and the young man superscibing them as mother and son. Mother - nineteen, son-twenty-four years old !

All burst into laughter. That night Nisha and Sheila enjoyed a sound sleep but Anshupa had not a wink of sleep. At times she woke up and then fell on bed motionless. Chhayanidhi's face writhing in pain flashed in her inward eye; clutching his belly, he was groaning "Mother, Mother" Anshupa felt extremely restless as she perceived him to be genuine. Motherhood in her was irresistibly overpowering.

- Was she Chhayanidhi's mother, really ! The question tore her into pieces. She woke up, looked around and found Nisha and Sheila fast asleep. She thought to wake them up to chat with them about Chhayanidhi but restrained herself. Drank a tumbler of water and retired to bed. She wished Chhyanidhi were a fraud as it would be grievous if he was true. She prayed to God to make her father's words come true. She felt as though the computers on her front asking," Why do you believe in Chhayanidhi in this age of information technology, computer, wireless, life on other planets, cloning, intra-sexuality, etc ?

She turned quizzical and answered herself, "Why should fetishness, divination, a person divinely possessed, rebirth,   previous birth, parapsychology be impossible in this age of   incredibly unprecedented inventions? Maybe these constitute the next phase of science which man now considers incredible and impossible." She remembered the guest scientist's address in the college seminar, "Our knoweldge of the universe is just like a grain of sand on a vast beach. Above all the 'soul' is the greatest blessing for man. Far beyond scientific knowledge; knowledge of the soul gets man rid of diminutive science."

She switched on the zero power bulb, put out the balcony light, sat in a chair, and dwelt upon Chhayanidhi again

-What's wrong if he were her son in the previous birth! But the problem is - why should he eat her leftovers? Why serve her? Had he killed his mother or driven her out in her old age, so that she died at a roadside? Is this the cause of his suffering from colic in this birth? What harm, if he believes that he can be cured by taking my leftovers, Anshupa turned pendulous and failed to accept the thought she harboured. Besides, Chhayanidhi was a young man, older than her. People might read into it and decry her credulity. They might demand a proof of his being her son and spread calumny that she was romancing with him. The entire Engineering College, nay the entire town would fuss about it. An engineering student, though, she hailed from a village. She was not completely free from its culture. Moreover she was very much obsessed with typical middle class prudery. No, Chhayanidhi was a dupe, a swindler. Ruffled, she walked back from the balcony and slept.

On later days she was normal, Chhayanidhi intruded her psyche no more. Unusually mystifying and mysterious though, such occurrence found no room in her hectic life. It became flimsy, fragile and frusty.

Fifteen days later. About four o'clock in the afternoon. Informed by the watchman, Anshupa and her companions went outside the hostel gate. A man over fifty was standing. He had put on an ordinary peice of dhoti. He had grizzled moustache. He was visibly restless. Anshupa scrutinized him from top to toe and asked. "Who do you look for ?"

- Anshupa Behera, he replied.

- What for ?

- I shall tell her - humbly he said.

- I am Anshupa Behera, tell me your problem. She expressed with a pinch of harshness.

The fellow looked at her searchingly. Hands folded, he said, 'Mother, did my Chhayanidhi come to you ?'

Anshupa and her friends were taken aback as Chhayanidhi's image flashed across their minds.

- Who is he ? asked Ansupa in no time,

Chhayanidhi's father stared at her, his face pathetically contorted. He asked, "Didn't a person suffering from colic meet you ?"

- No. Sternly replied she, while her companions did not buzz even.

- He is my son; he had left home to meet you fifteen days back, not yet returned. No information about him I have got. The man heaved a deep sigh and looked at her.

Maintaining studied silence about Chhayanidhi,

Anshupa returned to her room with her friends.She sat in a chair and drank a glass of water as Sheila said, "Lo ! what a piece of magic again !"

Anshupa smiled and then the three turned grave. Sheila offered them mixture and munched a morsel of it. "Should we journey to Chhayanidhi's village to unravel the truth ? An adventure, of course," she said excitedly.

Ansupa became thoughtful.Sheila continued "Look, we are getting disturbed again and again. Uncle also didn't let us know what his messenger collected about Chhayanidhi. At first appeared Chhayanidhi, then his father. Then his brother and his uncle would come". She stopped as she found that Ansupa was perplexed.

-Let us not react now. If anyone comes hereafter, we must take him to task, said Nisha.

Anshupa phoned to her father, 'Hello, Father ! Did you get the whereabouts of Chhayanidhi, that colic patient ?'

- No, nothing could I get to know about the village of the goddess he referred to. Well, did he go to you again ?

-No, but his father came here in search of him. He returned disappointed as we informed him that we did n't know him - said Ansupa.

- Do you face any more trouble ? Moti babu asked

- No, father.

- Should I go to you? He asked her in a wearied voice.

- No, we are ok. Be not worried. In case, any trouble arises I shall phone you. Ansupa turned off her phone.

Sheila caught hold of her and said, "We were brave enough to scare away a man with a patent lie."

- "Who knows, both father and son are deceptive. Maybe the father came to convince us that his son was really a colic patient. Nothing impossible," said Nisha.

- I care a fig for the colic patient. Hundreds are dying of diseases everyday. Who cares ? Saying so Anshupa entered her bathroom.

Next day afternoon. They hired an auto to go for shopping. Before they entered the Supermarket, they found Chhayanidhi rolling on ground in excruciating pain. With a bottle of water in hand, his father was pressing his belly. Ansupa asked the auto driver to stop there. They got down the auto and saw from a distance Chhayanidhi rolling in pain.

- Chhayanidhi has not left the town since then - Sheila said

- And his pain is genuine - said Nisha.

- The person near him is his father. Not an impersonating father - Said Ansupa.

They entered the Supermarket for shopping.

Time passed. No untoward incident happened in Ansupa's life though at times Chhayanidhi's contorted face danced in her momeny as once it was the experience of a rare event . However, she felt much pain. But she did not meet Chhayanidhi till her studies were over. At times she would repent for calling Chhayanidhi a hypocrite. But what else could she have done except doing that ? Sheila got married and Nisha was going to join a company job this month. She too was happy that she would mary a scientist next month. Her family was busy preparing for the nuptial bliss. She was asking them to buy her apparel and ornament as per her choice.

Ansupa's wedding day. She has already come on the altar. The auspicious hour is drawing nigh and the entire atmosphere is surcharged with festivity - all are in an indulgent mood. The pipers are blowing pipes. The sacrificial fire is burning on the altar. Ansupa now looks like an empress adorned in marriage crown on her head. The articles needed for the ceremony are on the altar. The priest is chanting hymns. Near her is Aniket in groom's gorgeous attire. At the appointed moment the priest unites their hands in a knot to the blowing of conches, beating of drums and piping of pipes. The elders present around the altar sprinkle sacred rice and flowers gleefully on them as a token of blessing.

The priest goes on chanting hymns and asks Aniket to repeat it. As Aniket does, at a point Ansupa senses something and requests the priest in a subdued voice to chant the hymn again and explain its meaning. The priest explains," O, woman! You may be my mother or sister in previous birth but I take you as my wife with an oath before this sacred fire, in this birth."

Ansupa is startled, her entire body getting sensitive. The scene of Chhayanidhi rolling on footpath clasping his belly, groaning in pain and addressing mother flashes in her inward eye.

Tears well up in her eyes. Her quivering lips spurt out "Chhaya............"

■

The Lover

Warbling, Satura was way home. The sun was about to set. He was not far from home on his way back from Anantapur. Just six miles away. For fifteen long years he was doing this. Carrying food items or any other necessary things to the people's relatives living at far off places. Indeed his readiness to do this made him everyone's cynosure.

Satura was forty. Frail and dwarfish. A man fondly requisitioned for everyone's chores on festive occasions. He was well acquainted with his villagers' relatives and friends. With an all –embracing attitude he would glorify their relatives. His eulogy was so superlative, in a flourish of language bordering on fiction.

- Lo, your relative, what a man! Fed me with delicious dishes befitting the elite. Fish, various curries, sweets, what not! Really wonderful"

He would never forget to sing the panegyrics of his own locality in amazing hyperboles. Satura formed a bridge between people and their relatives. A marvellous feat indeed!

Suave and naive, he could endear himself to all and sundry. On festivals like Durga Puja, Holi, Raja, etc. people would want Satura to carry their things to their friends and relatives. Satura's cup of joy would reach its brim. He would be overwhelmed with their insistence and entreaty. However, he used to comply on a first come, first served basis. Very much capricious, he was instinctive and credulous too. His voice, a little bit piping. Generous in paying for things. Often more than their price. People took him to be a muddle-head. He breathed free in spite of self-inflicted discomfort and troubles caused to himself due to his naiveté'. Yet he would remain impervious to them.

But, he would turn stultified and stumbled for an answer when asked about his family. A lava of torment seemed to sear into his heart. He felt hollow. Tears trickled down his cheeks to the shock and surprise of the questioner. Benumbed, he would feel like offering his sympathies to Satura. Satura would then leave the place crestfallen and sullen.

He had left his village, Sunapur, fifteen years back, ignoring his kith and kin, hearth and home. There, he belonged to a Pradhan family. His father had two sons, Santia and Satura and a daughter who was married off before the old man's death. The old Pradhan too had incurred much debt to meet Santia's marriage expenses. However, before death he could repay all the loans. He had left behind eight acres of alluvial land for sons.

Satura turned more reverent towards his elder brother and sister in law after father's departure. He considered them to be his parents. Never went against whatever they commanded him. For his brother, he would do anything ... he could climb mountains indeed. His brother was his dearest. No less was his sister in law's filial love for him. The lady, having no child yet showered all her affection on the slightly quaint Satura, her only brother-in-law and cherished him.

Just after a year of his father's death, Satura got married. Lo, what a girl he got! A Paragon of beauty who stole everyone's heart in no time. But strangely she left for her father's house disgruntled, only a month after her marriage. She complained to her cousins against her husband's apathy towards her. His brother and sister in law were his sole concern, she added. Frankly she declined to stay with such a blockhead. She preferred death to living with such a creature.

Since then Satura's world turned topsy-turvy. The sonorous stream of his life metamorphosed into a raucous cascade.

He married again six months later. Rejuvenated, he turned over a new leaf. Life was now roses and roses, all the way. But the second stint at conjugal life also nosedived four months after marriage. One day, after hours of hard labour in cornfields, Satura returned home in haste, exhausted to the core.

It was midday. He deposited the pickaxe on the veranda of the cowshed. He was about to cross the threshold of the middle door. He was taken aback to find his brother's room closed from inside though his brother's wife had been to her father's.

Satura halted at the door speechless and listened to the ominous conversation between his brother and his wife. Giddiness overtook him completely. Amorous whispers accompanied by romantic chuckles from inside the room whizzed past his ears and whittled him away.

- "Don't worry, I own everything—the house and the landed property. I shall see that the bloody fool leaves the village"- His brother whispered into his wife Tulasi's ears.

- "If he knows about our relationship ….? She queried.

- "No,no, how will that dullard know ? Even if he knows, he will keep mum. Otherwise I shall thrash him or ...."

- "Or ..?" She asked.

-" Finish him off while asleep."

Satura could fathom the conspiracy. An inexplicable torrent of shock ran down his spine. Tears wet the ground under his feet, tears betokening his reverence for his brother. Without delay he set out,traversing miles after miles. At last he reached here, Jhandasahi, where he had spent fifteen summers.

Jhandasahi was a place thirty miles from his native village Sunapur. Time has worn him out turning his hair white. Nobody neither his kith and kin, nor his brother has ever enquired about him since then.

Dusk ... Satura reached his modest hut on the outskirts of the village. Kept at a side the bamboo- plank used to carry things on his shoulder. Then he called out: "Hello my dear, open the door. I am totally exhausted. So much work, do you hear?"

A while later he continued: "Why are you silent, are you suffering from fever? What a pity! How I wish you massaged my tired limbs. Let me not grumble since you are unwell".

He unlocked the door and entered. Lighted a lamp. Pulled out of his bag, four new rings of earthen bracelets. Brimming joyfully he burst out- "See, how dainty these are! Tell me, do you like them? Upon my name, be frank. O, why don't you speak? I see, fever is the cause. I shall not worry you. Let me light the hearth, fetch water. Then I shall attend upon you. Put on the bracelets around your wrists. O, yes, let me cook rice for you first."

At this moment Nari master called him again and again from outside. A pitcher in hand, Satura came out.

"Hello, my boy, to-day I learnt about a hidden truth. You have never broached the subject. It's good you got married. You are lonely no more. Really you have beautified the house. But I am confused; tell me when was the wedding solemnised?" Nari master said.

Satura listened to him, mute and crestfallen. Completely forlorn.

Nari master queried again, "Why don't you answer me? Are you bashful about it?"

Bisia Jena, a neighbour, approached the master and asked, "What's the matter?"

"About Satura's marriage. I just want to know when he got married. Nothing more."

" Sir, why do you think Satura is married?"

"I was outside his hut. Heard his dalliance with his wife. Satura told his wife to put on the bracelet, and even he comforted her saying that he will attend upon her as she was ailing. A very happy couple indeed! They will face no misery in life."

Nari master laughed heartily while Satura stood sepulchral.

Bisia led the master inside to see the bride. But the latter seemed not interested in coming forward as she was unwell.

Bisia insisted and Nari Master entered the room totally nervous. Satura stayed out. Nari Master in the dimly-lit light, saw a fully wrapped woman asleep. Notwithstanding the master's repeated cautioning, Bisia pulled out the sheet to Nari's stupefaction.

- "What is it !" Nari couldn't believe his eyes. Not a woman, but a "Pakhia!" (palm leaf made article used as umbrella by the rural peasant at the time of cultivation, especially in rainy season. It resembles a human being in shape). Wrapped up neatly, it resembled a sleeping woman. Struck dumb, Nari master fumbled, "bracelets for this Pakhia.. !"

He found Satura weeping inconsolably. With a touch of emotion, he called him. Satura felt awfully overwhelmed with tidal tears.

His real life was in tatters fifteen years back. Now his fancy was no better, the fancy very much his own had been caught and unveiled by others.

Nari Master requested Satura to carry sweets, fruits and vegetables to his pregnant daughter at Sunapur. Like an apparition, Tulasi was haunting Satura. He reminisced her romantic way of addressing him: "How sweet you are, dear...!" Those words shook him to the core. He felt their sledge- hammer blow pounding on his chest still.

Distance and difficulties notwithstanding, he agreed to go to Sunapur after some initial reluctance and dithering. A spasm of enthusiasm of visiting his brother swirled him.

He reached his native village in the evening. However, instead of feeling elated he felt lackadaisical and was gripped with fright. Terrible indeed! His village failed to console him; rather it spread a blanket of disillusion all around. What an irony! Gathering himself, he drank deep the country panorama even though for a moment. He felt sandwiched between identity and its loss.

His dramatic arrival made the villagers throng around him. Their volley of questions concerning his present whereabouts, his condition, wearied him. The village folk told him they had known about his wife's affair resulting in his abandoning home, then his committing suicide in the river. Some even said they thought he had been killed by his brother.

Satura heard them patiently but straightway proceeded towards Nari Master's daughter's house. Delivered the sweets etc. to her family and busied himself listening to the old woman of the house about the village affairs. She related everything threadbare .... how Santia made Tulasi his concubine ... the rumours about his murder by his brother ...... how the villagers were opposed to Santia .... who fathered as many as nine children by his two wives. And how Tulasi had died three years ago unable to deliver the last child.

She continued with her narration ...that things did not go well after he left home. Santia suffered from rheumatism and turned a lame duck. His family life went down like ninepins, two wives always at loggerheads with each other, a large family banking upon him and to cap it all, continuous floods compelling him to sell out his landed property to sustain the family. Neck deep in debt and crop failure made the Pradhan family almost a cadaver.

Satura heard it all without a blink, though disinterested. But the moment he heard his brother suffering from fever for a week, he broke down emotionally. All his sulk melted in the air. He rushed to meet him.

Santia clasped him sobbing nonstop.

- O, my brother dear ! I am the most ignoble sinner. It's good you have come back. People accused me of killing you. Now the truth is out and I am saved. Do tell me, where had you been ?

Satura stood, tears welling up in his eyes. His sister-in-law held him fondly and in a voice choked with emotion she wept and wept relating the children's misery. He could not return to Jhandasahi and stayed back. Arranged medical treatment for his brother and took charge of cultivation too. At times, however, he felt an ache, a pang, inexplicable. He also recognized that he had a sense of hatred along with love for Tulasi's children.

One night he felt tormented with gnawing loneliness. Tulasi's words, "How sweet you are, Darling" nibbled at him deceptively. Wounded, he would remember while in bed, his brother's words of conspiracy. Frightening.

Restlessness led to sleeplessness. Some days he spent this way. Santia recovered from illness by degrees. Now, he was able-bodied. One morning Santia's wife asked Satura, "You seem worried and sleepless. Why? Do you feel the pang of separation from your sweet heart at Jhandasahi?

Satura smiled.

Next day, he finished his morning duties, ate rice gruel and held his bamboo plank. Santia asked, "Where are you going?"

"Jhandasahi".

"What for?"

Satura had no words and he stood motionless. Santia and his wife felt deep sorrow. Their children clasped their uncle. Satura assured them "Don't worry, I shall be back. Yes I shall come back. Now I must return to meet Nari master because I had been here for his work. He must have been worried now as I did not return in time. I may go now, but I will certainly come back. More over, she was suffering from fever".

"Who is she? Suffering from fever? Asked his sister in law.

"O, Yes, she is suffering….. let me be off"…..

"I must come back, must, Good bye …"..

Bowing down his head at his sister-in-law's feet, Satura came out, flushed.

■

The Golden Jackal

The old haggard, Kangali peered at the sky from his scaffolding in his orchard near the river bank. Pitch darkness all around. An awful night besieged by tormenting solitude. The sky hypnotised him beyond measure. Kangali's eyes twitched. He forgot he was away from his village. As if he turned into a stream of consciousness.

Wonderful indeed! He cogitated. Man-tiny, a veritable speck in the vast universe, apprehensive, perplexed and worn- out. Yet, through the ages nature has played first fiddle to rescue him from the conundrums of crises. Man has surveyed its mighty presence rapturously. It has energised him too.

Kangali's fancy shot through the sky. He felt a biting chill across his spine.... Lo, man's trip to planets, his launching of rockets into space! What a tragedy it would be if one such rocket got crashed into this scaffolding !

He whizzed in fanciful gyration. Alarmed too, he withdrew his head into the haystack shed. Smoked a birland inspected all around.

All well..... his weapons ready to meet with any untoward situation – a bamboo pole and a javelin. Besides, the lantern had fuel to its fill. He felt relieved. The place has been his safe shelter during nights in the last three years. So he has been able to yield bumper crop and vegetables.

In fact, he had made the scaffolding to be on vigil to prevent theft. Three years back burglars robbed him of all fruits and vegetables grown there. Since then he started playing sentinel at night. So he kept the weapons to thwart any such misadventure. The javelin and the bamboo staff apart, he kept small slabs of stone too. He would throw one such if he heard any mysterious sound at night. So the wild animals would be scared away. At times he would throw a slab of stone without rhyme and reason. It would fall into water and make a splash or else it would create some sound if it struck against the leaves of a tree. Kangali would sport a warm smile spreading along his mouth like a maiden moon. As a result, the smoke emitted by the "biri"- stick would belch out.

Kangali felt ill at ease in the silence of the night. It seemed the world was dead as it were. Sound, verily signifies man's existence. Kangali's cup of joy rose to its brim the moment he heard jackals howl. In a state of frenzied excitement he would repeat their howl. The jackals too would prolong their howl as if to compete with him like the cuckoo prolonging its cooing when children imitate it. It transported Kangali to a paroxysm of ecstasy. After such mimicry he felt benumbed- the villagers might ridicule him for such a childish prank.

The dead of night, quite somber and awesome. Kangali would wind a napkin around his head, anoint his heels with oil, make his lantern glow dimly and fall asleep covering himself with a blanket. Just then a jackal would howl and he felt a pang of despair. The number of jackals dwindled day by day. And the villagers whispered-'Lo, there's a golden jackal in Kangali's orchard. Any seed he plants, never remains unyielded - pumpkin, brinjal, lemon, chilly, cucumber, mango; what not! Yah..!" But he had nobody to enjoy all such. The night would get intense; Kangali would hear some weird sound on the banks of the river and throw a slab of stone.

Memories zoomed in, making him sleepless…. In youth he was employed as a jute mill worker in Calcutta. He had his wife Parbati and son Rabi with him there. A year after, he smelled a rat behind the mill supervisor Kishan's assigning him night duty invariably. He was taken aback on an afternoon when he found Parbati mysteriously vanishing leaving Rabi asleep near him. He tried his best to find her out but in vain. In fear of shame he did not lodge an FIR with the police nor could he broach the matter to anyone. Days after, he got news Parbati was staying with Kishan. Tears trickled down his cheeks. He clasped his child. He found nothing wanting in him so that Parbati should cast him aside. Alas ! she too could forget her child ! Sulking, he returned to his native village with the child. There he did not divulge the shameful matter. However, he told the villagers that Parbati died of cholera.

Memory……. Kangali felt tremulous. Excitement ran down his spine. To break the impenetrable silence he pelted another pebble that made a splash in the river water.

Oh…….. he felt relieved as things were all right, But, he could not get a wink of sleep.

Rabi grew up, studied up to class seven to his éclat. But one day he too in his youth set out for Calcutta even though Kangali forbade. Kangali apprehended he might meet his mother accidentally. The matter would turn worse as Rabi had been told of his mother's demise due to cholera at Calcutta.

Rabi got a job in a Bengali family and fell in love with its widow having elephantine foot. Neck deep in her love, he forgot his father. A desperate Kangali rushed to him to wean him away. But to no purpose. Once the widow had chased him away menacingly. Eyes welled up in tears and he returned.

Now he experienced death in life, a man sandwiched between hope and despair. He was in no man's land, a man who would ascend his scaffolding and descend to the earth. He had amassed a lot of gold in a box under the earth. Rabi might return one day, and enjoy the fruit of his labour. But Rabi never returned keeping him on tenterhooks of optimism.

Kangali kept the match box near his head, groped for the javelin and the bamboo stick and put out the lantern. Night grew deep, earth getting cooler. All at once he heard somebody calling him out. He turned more alert and clasped his javelin.

- Hello, who are you? Why do you call out from the corn fields in late night? – He responded in a loud voice.

No reply,…. An unnerved Kangali repeated his query to no purpose. He heard a mysterious rustle at the nearby screw-pine bush. He threw pebbles at the sound. Again a rustle, again he threw pebbles. His heart palpitated faster, "Maybe a thief had come to loot my orchard. Maybe he wants to ascertain if I was asleep or awake. That's why he called out."

He felt restless and petrified, took the ladder up the scaffolding. Now he was agitated. No use of throwing pebbles, it's time to use the javelin for self- defence, he decided at last. He heard the sound again and threw the javelin at the screw - pine bush. A terrible shriek of pain of a wounded jackal he heard. Kangali felt shaky and shocked apprehending the mystifying golden Jackal's death-the animal attributed to be the cause of his bumper harvest in his orchard. Very much at his wits' end and perspiring, he wished to see if the animal was dead. But bouts of fear prevented him from descending the platform. A deadly silence all around pierced him. He was dumbstruck. Frozen in fear too. As if misfortune spread its tentacles around him! He turned frantic and continued throwing stones nonstop. He felt elated with each stone producing some sound. It consoled and rose his spirit. He felt sure of his existence. Sound, indeed is a means to exert one self and know oneself.

In the wee hours, he got down his shelter and in a sleepy state approached the tragic spot, and found a jackal dead. The javelin had pierced its heart. Its blood had stained the spot. Kangali shrank in pity and fear. He burst into tears, uncontrollably. In fear of being criticised by the villagers, he lifted it and paced onward hastily. Across the threshold of his house, he saw a slumbering old woman in white. Kangali stared at her.

- Well, who are you ?

The old woman woke up, looked at him intently, and sobed inconsolably…..

- Where is my son? She asked him.

- What do you mean?

- Yes, my son Rabi!

Kangali was taken aback; he experienced an earthquake ….Oh, you ! …. he got overwhelmed.

Parbati unravelled her tale of woe.

"Yes, I am your Parbati whom the Bihari Kisan enticed and enjoyed for six months. Then he sent her to a brothel where she grew old." Heavy with a lump in her throat, she sobbed.

It dawned. In a state of quandary, Kangali cursed himself. How wretched I am! People will take me a liar. What did I do?"

- Did you call me out last night?

The old woman replied in the negative, "I found your house locked. No way out. Hence I took rest on the verandah."

Kangali felt nonplussed, immediately threw away the dead jackal and opened the door.

- Haven't you got married again? Where is Rabi? Parbati queried.

Kangali breathed a deep sigh and told her about Rabi's tragedy.

She got emotioned –"Please let me meet my son, at least once, please arrange! Or else take me to Culcutta to visit him"- She insisted.

Kangali got dressed in no time and told her – Guard my gold underneath the earth here. I shall leave no stone unturned to see that Rabi returns. But what shall I tell him? Earlier I told him that you were dead. Now how can I tell that leaving me you eloped with someone? Is it so easy to make a lie a lie? A Gordian knot indeed.

Parbati stared and stared. She discovered a Christ in Kangali.

- Listen, don't go to the farmyard, the dead jackal's body is there, yes, the golden jackal!

Kangali finished his caution, handed over the lock and key to Parbati, and strode towards the railway station in seclusion. Much, much before the sunrise.

Rabi returned a few days later, but not Kangali. The carcass of the jackal was already stinking.

■

The Cave

VIGNETTES OF A FORGETTABLE STORY

SCENE:ONE

Saint Bhadra Devi lived in an impenetrable cave of Ramagiri Hills. Nobody knows since when she has been there. She was bright and white-haired; her eyes closed, her attire white, face smiling. Light failed to penetrate the cave adequately yet it was not dark altogether.

She sat on a slab of stone of square size. It was past afternoon. Firing was heard very near. The cave trembled as it experienced an explosion. The saint's meditation broke. Yet there was no trace of surprise, fear, or anxiety on her visage. She could absorb all such violent sound. All on a sudden a person with a rifle entered her cave. A shot from outside pierced him when he was busy firing. He fell down; blood oozing from his chest reddened the floor. Bhadra Devi got a bit ruffled; she went near the dead and examined his nostrils and hand to ascertain if he was alive. She drew a deep breath, returned to her sitting place and closed eyes for meditation.

Another gun-wielding person ran to that place instantly and felt glad as he saw the dead gunman. His face exuded happiness just as a line of lightning in the rainy season flashing in the sky.

-Your long-trodden road is over, Yuganad! He uttered and spat on the dead.

Then his attention was drawn towards an old woman sitting on a slab of stone. Astonished, he approached her and asked, "Well, who are you?"

He had seen saints and seers inhabiting caves of hills. But how come a solitary woman doing meditation in an area of terrorists! He wondered. Was she a terrorist? their saviour? He thought and waited for the old woman's answer.

As no reply came, he turned grave and excited too. – "Now you answer me. I am a commander, fighting with terrorists. If you don't reply, I shall imprison you or even shoot you." He thundered.

The old woman remained nonchalant. Rather her face shone brighter as if to mock at the commander. Or even it challenged him as it were. The enraged commander pointed his revolver at her and shouted, "You have already made me impatient. I ask you for the last time: Who are you? What's your identity? Tell it soon..."

His shout reversed in the cave. Yet the old woman remained unruffled.

Now the commander's eyes turned red. He was about to shoot but stopped. What use killing a saintly woman ! The saint tradition of thousands years of human civilization danced before him. But in his front there was a woman appearing mysterious! He thought, "Is this silent, saintly woman more powerful than I?" He questioned himself and put his revolver in the sheath. Knelt down before her and said earnestly, "Dear Mother! I bow to you. I am an army official. The responsibility of safety of the country has been entrusted to me. Please help me discharge my duties. Please disclose your identity."

Even then the saintly old woman did not break her meditation.

-Dear mother! How can you meditate if the place is not safe?So our duty is worthy. I simply desire to know who you are.

The threat of revolver and humility of request were same for her. She remained impervious to these.

Heaving a deep breath, the Commander looked around with the eye of an eagle. He stared at the dead terrorist again and kicked his buttock. When he was about to go outside the cave, the old woman from behind said, "Listen Commander!"

The Commander halted and the affectionate voice appeared to be a mother's for her son, he felt. He looked back and stood before her in attention position. Strange! How could I behave like an obedient person before an unknown saintly old woman when she did not budge ever after so many questions and so much wait? He wondered.

-Listen.I didn't call you back to give you my identity. But I want to make you aware of the crime you committed. Said she.

-My crime! The Commander interjected.

-You spat on the dead man you killed. It's a crime, she said.

-He is not an individual; he is a hard core terrorist.

-Is he still a terrorist even after death? She questioned.

-Dear saintly Mam! One's identity is not lost even after one's death. He was a terrorist before death and so is after, the Commander said emphatically.

-Then what's your identity? The Commander who kicks and spits? Right? Of course, one's identity is susceptible to changes. You will remain as a retired Commander after your service is over but couldn't command. Spitting on a dead person or kicking him is not the identity of a patriot. You should be punished for such crime. Somewhere someday.

Her words pierced the Commander. He kept mum for a while and then shouted, "Damn! You plead for an extremist!"

-One gets bewildered when one realizes one's crime. Now you are in that state. Tapaswini said.

The Commander didn't reply, cast an angry look at her, and came out of the cave.

SCENE : TWO

The dusk was approaching.Tapaswini sat in her seat, her eyes closed. Four soldiers entered the cave and carried away the dead extremist. Darkness spread in the cave by degrees. It was dawn again. A read ball emerged on the mountain Ramagiri. As a result, the inside of the cave was lighted flimsily. A beautiful woman clad in white sari entered the cave with a basket.

Depositing the basket on a slab of stone she knelt down and touched the saint reverentially. Her touch didn't affect the saint or the latter simply minced such touch deliberately; It couldn't be deciphered because the saint's meditation didn't break.

The woman got up, looked all around again. She guessed there was none except the old saint absorbed in deep meditation in a cave in a mountain in a dense forest. That too silently! She was surprised.

-Revered Mother! Please open eyes;I am here to beg pardon to you. She expressed with considerable modesty.

The saint opened eyes, smiled at the stranger just as a mother takes her girl child to her lap. Her behaviour changed the aristocratic gravity of the woman into an intimacy. Tears welled up in her eyes. She said, 'Mother! My husband misbehaved with you yesterday. He repents for that and I have come to beg apology since he has gone to a distant place on an urgent transaction. I heard everything from him, felt his remorse. Hence I came here. Indeed, he admits he committed a mistake by spitting on and kicking the dead body of an extremist. Please forgive him!"

-Now you look like a person begging forgiveness. But why you beg it? You have not committed the crime.

The woman was taken aback, Now she was changed by the naïve smile of the saint! Yes, it is possible for a saint. If one embraces transformation, one can transform the environment.

-O Mother! Did you forgive my husband? She implored.

-He is repenting, all right. He should forgive himself first. It is true, he would be begging forgiveness to himself throughout his life, She said.

The lady asked her anxiously: Mother! A lot of questions arise in my mind as I find you doing penance solitarily. Would you please bless me with answers?

-O, yes; You could listen but would fail to realize, because you don't have that power. You may go now. Your companions are waiting for you worriedly outside the cave.

The lady was taken aback. How could the saint know she had come with security guards! She bowed her head reverently.

-Don't be surprised. How can a commander's wife come without retinue? I am sure someday you would get answers to the questions arising in you now.

The lady returned with a sense of humility. And the saint vanished.

SCENE : THREE

: Bhadra! Someone called in a mild tone.

The sage, who stood on her right foot with the left leg resting on the right knee and her hands raised upward completely and eyes closed in a reverential posture sprang in surprise. She opened her eyes and discontinued her yogic position.

She looked around and waited silently. Sound of shoes was audible clearly.Bhadra exuded a mysterious laugh. Whether it was of satire or delight or derision or of love, couldn't be known. An old man of robust health stood in her front; his eyes still emitting fire. The pair of pant and shirt of faint green colour he put on was soiled at places. A revolver was visible in his pocket.

-Why did you come again? Bhadra asked.

-I couldn't help coming. Swayam, the old man, replied.

-What sort of infatuation is it?

-Just a meeting, exchange of a few words. That's all.

-Don't distrub my penance any more. Just you know that this should be our last meeting. Otherwise I will change the place. Bhadra expressed very calmly but stubbornly.

What do you say, I am disturbing you? You are intimate to me for the last thirty years. Can you delete that memory? You are not free from that memory but you say that this short meeting perturbs you! Swayam said.

- Do you comprehend the meaning of my penance? Yes, I would have erased that memory, but I didn't want. I have kept it half-covered and half-open. And I shall erase all of it after this meeting, just as one's memory is lost due to an accident. The way you still hold onto is getting stopped due to the evolution of nature. But you are still excited.

As the saint vented this at a stretch, Swayam trembled

in fury and shouted: "Stop it". His shout echoed in the cave and melted. He heaved a deep sigh again and again. Sat on the stone and said, "Well, I came to see you. I quenched that thirst. Now I depart." He stood up.

The saint asked instantly: Where is our son?

-I don't know. Swayam answered.

-Well, even your idealism failed to attract him!

-True.

-Learn from this, one is not tied to an ideal always nor does an ideal draw all to its fold.

-I admit. But Bhadra, an ideal is capable enough to attract some for all time to come.

As Bhadra remained silent, he continued, "You left me and my ideals; did penance for years together. But what's accrued?

Bhadra chuckled. Whether Swayam could fathom it, was not read.

-Well, please show me the result of your prolonged struggle, said she.

Swayam too smiled mildly and said that he would depart.

-Did you not try to know about our son's whereabouts? Bhadra asked anxiously.

-No. Said Swayam.

-Please, don't come here again. She said sternly.

-I shall try. But I get terribly upset if I don't see you. Every moment you…..

The saint interrupted, "See, for so many years we have parted. You have your way, I mine, different. Is your idealism so fragile as to rectify your weakness so that you are running to me again and again?"

-You are doing penance. Yet you too are not free from filial attachment. Swayam cast an irony.

-O, I see. Then you have perceived the difference between affection and attachment; she curtly said.

Since his arrival here Swayam was looking inquisitively around at times and heaving a deep sigh.

-He, whom you are in quest has felled to bullets and his corpse has been taken away by soldiers. Bhadra said.

Bewildered, Swayam looked at her. He thirsted for so much wonder, so many moments gone by, so much sacrifice and so much rebellion in her eyes.

The excitement of spring
The chilly evening of winter
The dew drops of autumn
Bra, bikini, swimming pool
Union of lips.
And
The footpath along metropolis
Refugees, hamlets, and shanties
Trade of tins of blood and flesh
Sniggers of the broker
Saliva of the fiend.
And
Oath by the flag
History clandestine.

Drops of innumerable experiences in the four eyes!

All on a sudden firing was heard all around the cave and the sound drew nigh gradually.

Their eyes turned unstable. And they came to senses. Bhadra pulled Swayam's hands and they retired to a dark, inner chamber while firing sounded around.

Four armed soldiers saw an old woman in warrior's uniform, a gun in hand. They surrounded her. Just then their commander entered and said, "O, You! You are the saint I had met earlier on an operation here. But you were clad in the apparel of a saint then. Yet I suspected you and now the truth has come out.

The saint handed over her pistol to the commander.

SCENE:FOUR

Swayam didn't flee the cave in Ramagiri hill. Instead he was found sitting in meditation on the stony floor there. After a little while he rose, became distressed and loitered here and there. How Bhadra could practise meditation on such a stony floor for so many years, he wondered.

He calmed down himself. Unless one feels thirsty one can't dabble in it whether sports, literature, dance, music, commerce, love, revolution or meditation. Did Bhadra really absorb herself in meditation and connect herself with something? He cogitated. Connect with what? He connected himself with the dream of equality of all men. All must have equal rights, none would exploit anyone, and no body would exert their supremacy over any one. Revolution, struggle and going underground, all these for that only.

Now what happened? Bhadra won but did not allow me to be defeated. Rather she offered an opportunity. Where's gone the enthusiasm, fervour, excitement, creating storm and commitment to encounter that had gripped him thirty years before! Am I to enter that array of democracy now against which I had raised voice? Should I be its captive at last? With what social process do the human psyche and the world go now? Would the struggle for its fulfilment continue till it happens in course of the evolution?

Swayam drew a deep sigh, sat on a slab of stone, and looked at the cave above and below. Light penetrated through a small hole in the corner. He looked at the light intimately and intently. His eyes sparkled. He had not fathomed Bhadra's words that day. Now he could comprehend what she had expressed, "Sages are as busy as you are. Through penance energy turns undulating being concentrated. That results in acceleration of the evolutionary process. Your revolution, my penance…..their consummate realization is not attainment of liberation."

Swayam drooped to vacillation again. He stood up and wandered here and there. He saw only that cave, and a hole in one of its corners.

He made a tempestuous exit from that place.

THE LAST SCENE

The police officer laughed. He had never laughed like this. The laughter had no rancour; it didn't register a sense of kindness. It was a deeply felt laughter of wonder.

Swayam looked at the police officer with a sense of surprise.

— "Well, to rescue you from being arrested Mrs Bhadra had surrendered in the cave putting on your uniform and wielding your gun. It is ok. You too also surrendered to release her. But Sir, it is not possible even though you have surrendered", said the police officer excitedly.

-What do you mean? Swayam asked.

-If she is released, you would flee for her breaking the boundary.

■

The Arrest

As he deposited himself in the chair of the officer in charge the day he joined, the Kadamba tree shot through the front window made him exclaim, "Should a Kadamba tree be on the campus of a police station?" But he got infatuated with its sparkling round flowers he glanced. It was his first appointment and he was excited beyond measure, otherwise he would have forgotten he sat there as an officer. His absorption broke as he heard footsteps of a havildar with a file in hand standing on the other side of the chamber.

-Come in, he said.

The havildar entered with a salute and put the file on the table which Meghasan opened. Then he looked at the havildar with a smile and nodded him to depart. As the latter withdrew, Meghasan's attention was drawn to the tree automatically again. The tree was turning into a challenge, he felt. Gravely he uttered 'Hm' and started stroking his moustache, grown with care. He had grown it carefully since he prepared to sit for the police service exam.while cultivating physical fitness. As per his research, a moustache without beard can magnify itself.

Just then the same question cropped up in him again, "Should there be a Kadamba tree on the campus of a police station?" He projected himself to the question and replied, "You can't magnetise me towards you tree. And my moustache is capable enough to negate your existence."

At once he heard 'sir' 'sir' uttered pathetically from inside the 'lock-up'. Infact, such voice is the feature of a police station. He knew it to be heard every moment there.

As Meghasan came out, one ASI and two constables ran to him. But he asked them to leave him and mind their own business. Then he circumambulated the compound slowly. And marked that the Kadamba tree was visible from all sides more or less. A spontaneous smile in his lips and face drove him back to his adolescence. He turned at that moment a mountainous spring of memory but got dried up in no time. Meghasan controlled and asked himself: "Are you a police officer or a researcher of the Kadamba tree?" He felt repentant as he had spent a lot of time thinking about that tree. He whisked himself away to his chamber, closed the front window to free himself from the sight of that tree, and occupied his chair.

He felt, as it were, the tree jesting, "Well Meghasan! Did you see how I was able to close the window of your chamber?"

He opened the window and attended to the files in his front. A constable dragged a young man of eighteen to him and said, "Sir, this fellow is accused that he breaks sand houses made by children on shore, intrudes people's orchards and muzzles twigs, branches and foliage of trees therein. Tears off buds too. For which he has been beaten black and blue many a time but to no affect. He is incorrigible. Even today he intruded into three persons' gardens and tore off six buds."

Meghasan surveyed him intently; he was thin, of brown colour and of about five and a half feet height. He exuded exuberant youthful vigour, his eyes twitching nonstop. The person was visibly unstable though he stood. At times he, too, wriggled. Maybe he suffered from some nerve disease. Meghasan asked him why he tore off buds.

-No, Sir, I haven't.

-Do you think the policeman speaks untruth ? he said.

-Sir, it's true the buds have been torn off but by another person. The constable caught a wrong man like me.

As Meghasan cast a questioning glance at the constable, the latter confirmed that he had seen the accused jumping over the gate of someone's garden.

Pat came the youngman's reply, "Sir, he hasn't seen me plucking buds. Does jumping over a gate mean plucking buds?"

-Sir, I caught him when he jumped. The mistress of the house was pointing at him showing he had plucked buds." The constable replied.

Meghasan turned grave. While he lifted his baton on the table, his eyes met the Kadamba tree. He felt benumbed for a moment, his face becoming composed. He put the baton on the table again and asked the young man to sit on the bench.

-Sir, I am hungry.

-Be off. Said Meghasan.

The young man started scurrying around the police station. But the moment he saw the Kadamba tree, his strides slowed down. He approched the tree, plucked a bud, threw it and ran away.

Meghasan and the constable saw it through the window.

-The fellow, a psycho indeed. He may be a challenge to us in future.Collect details about him, Meghasan asked the constable.

The constable nodded, desired to ask Meghasan about something but restricted himself and looked at him and the baton.

-Do you want to say anything? Meghasan asked.

-No, Sir. The constable replied and went to another room.

Meghasan sat in his chair and looked at the Kadamba tree again and again. He drank a glass of water, pressed his forehead with his fingers and started heaving deep sighs in his mouth. He took some time to regain normalcy.

He remained busy investigating different cases till five thirty. It was not yet dusk. Twilight. But the natural beauty of the evening was covered with a sheet of light of the burning electric bulbs. The police station was noisy as usual. Meghasan saw an old man passing by the Kadamba tree singing: Kadamba Malinam Krishna........!

-"Hello, gentleman, come here, please"- Meghasan called him.

As the old man heard him, he became silent, strode slowly to him and saluted.

-'Who are you!' Asked Meghasan.

-Sir, I am havildar Kisan Sing, retired three months ago.

-Well, are you here for anything?

-No, Sir. I have got all my retirement dues. I just came to meet my old colleagues here. The old man replied.

His simple gesture appealed to Meghasan. He called him into his chamber and made him seated in the chair in front of him. As Kisan sat, Meghasan looked at him deeply. The sturdy old man in white pant and shirt had grown white beard and moustache, his eyes large but affectionate. Did not look menacing in anger and foxy even when cynic. Wonderful eyes indeed ! Kisan's appearance infected him with its catholicity. Distance between the in charge officer and a retired havildar shrank and a cordial relationship was established between them.

-Well, while going, you sang a song that had one word, Kadamba- Meghasan said.

-O, yes Sir. It is "Kadamba malinam Krushna gyayante nasti durgati".This is the verse that comes to my mind, the moment I chance upon a Kadamba tree. I can't help reciting.

Meghasan heard it with absorption and asked, "How long you served here?"

-Since this police station was set up ten years slid. The old man answered.

-What about this Kadamba tree? Meghasan queried.

Kisan felt embarrassed - Why was the officer interested to know about the tree rather than the area, its surroundings, environment, crimes committed here and the criminals ?

He said, "Sir! The tree existed before the police station was set up. When the building was constructed the higher officer said not to uproot it as it looked beautiful. Hence it remained". He became effusive and in a slight louder voice added, "Yes Sir, after the police station was inaugurated, the Minister, the Secretary, the DG, the Collector stood beneath the tree and took their photograph. A copy of the photograph has been kept on the clip-board. You may see it."

-Is it?

-Yes Sir. Since you are new to the place, you haven't seen the clip-board. There are clippings of poems, short stories, and visual arts, photographs of scenes of acting, singing, and music by our departmental persons. Also your predecessor here Shefali Roy's poem is clipped there too- Kisan expressed enthusiastically.

Meghasan thoughtfully uttered 'Ok' and asked, "Tell me if the police station has been affected anyway by the tree?"

Kisan looked at Meghasan with suspicion, typical of the police-psyche. Why was the officer getting so inquisitive about the Kadamba tree? Did anything occur due to it?" Kishan's curiosity grew more and more to fathom the mystery that connected the tree with the officer. He turned clever to know this and added more epithets to the tree to make it tempting. The officer - bachelor, robust and captivating was capable enough to magnetise damsels. Was he ensnared by any such trap on the day he joined here so that he remained absorbed in the tree? Kisan got entangled in such questions and drew an angle of discussion towards that.

- Sir, the tree is as inalienably related to this police station as you got related with it the moment you arrived here. Your predecessor was poet Shephali Roy who was known by that name everywhere. She got so many prizes for her poetry. After she joined here, she published poems about the tree. She used to lead many hardcore culprits to the tree and would take their photographs there. Then she would present them with such photographs saying, "Look. How your photographs with the tree look more beautiful than yours with guns and bent billhooks."

Kishan continued.

- Sir, she used to behave this way. As her pranks reached the DCP, he visited the police station. Madam Shephali said, 'Sir, the world has changed. Why should we not venture to take recourse to novel formulas to deal with culprits?"

-"Certainly. Novel experiments are welcome but you must be prepared for any eventuality. So, be careful." With these words, the DCP went to the tree and took a selfie with it. This encouraged madam more. And she took her selfie in different poses with the tree every day.

Meghasan stared at Kisan from whom the history of the police station flowed. However, Kisan's facial expression changed a bit just as a river takes a turn and a tender twig hangs. He kept mum for a while and then said, "Sir, roses bloomed in the Kadamba tree!"

Eyes wide open with enthusiasm and excitement, Meghasan drew himself in lightning speed towards Kisan and asked, "What, roses bloomed in the Kadamba tree!"

-Yes Sir, that actually happened.

-What do you mean? Meghasan exclaimed with much more scepticism.

Even though the night grew the comely evening stayed put for them, as it were. Meghasan had no serious business to deal with except signing files though some minor events occurred within the limits of the police station.

-Sir, Shepheli Madam arrested Jambhira – a formidable youth , implicated in bank robbery, highway robbery, snatching of women's necklaces, earrings, exploding bombs and throwing eggs, and rotten tomatoes to disturb election meetings. She had to employ strategies and force to tackle him. Jambhira's arrest was a remarkable feat of this police station. Crowds flocked to see the untamable Jambhira. But the really interesting thing happened when Madam did not confine him in the lock-up but tied him to this Kadamba tree. When her senior officer asked her, she replied, she had turned the tree into a lock-up for the time being. Everyone was stunned - journalists, photographers, etc. When it rumoured that Shephali Roy used such magic just to advertise herself, thus squandered public wealth and time, she pleaded that she be given a chance to do something unusual. Democracy thrives on novelty and dynamism, she argued. Jambhira, tied to the tree, wriggled and breathed deeply. The onlookers intently looked at every part of his body and took his photograph and sent it to their friends' whatsapp.

Jambhira shouted: I am thirsty. A constable brought a tumbler of water. Shephali Madam took it from him and made Jambhira drink.Thirst quenched, Jambhira's nose exuded the fragrance of Kadamba flowers. His deep breath slowed, his glowing eyes twinkled in placidity and poise. He leaned himself against the tree as though he touched the threshold of another world. After a while he started dozing, his eyelids almost closed. The Kadamba tree emitted a loud laughter. Madam observed Jambhira through the window and felt exultant and exuberant with the success of her experiment.

Jambhira's slumber broke after a while. He shouted, "I am famished." As a constable tried to feed him with a slice of bread, he declined to swallow. Again he shouted that he was hungry. The constable did the same but to no purpose. Jambhira uttered, "Madam". Shephali came to him, fed him with bread, drank him water. Jambhira slept thereafter.

Jambhira was forwarded to court. The court turned abuzz as he was produced there. He was addressed as the "prisoner of the Kadamba tree" and these words filled everyone's eyes with astonishment and excitement. Jambhira had also entered the courtroom with Kadamba flowers. Then he was sent to prison. By the time he reached the prison, the expression "the prisoner of the Kadamba tree" had been transformed into "Kadamba prisoner". Though his original name was recorded, it acquired the popular name "Kadamba prisoner."

Supper was served to prisoners. While all the prisoners emptied their plates, a plate of food remained untouched. Hundreds of efforts turned futile to empty the plate. The jailor said, "Are you on hunger strike? Or inviting death? Take food!" Jambhira brought out the Kadamba flower from his pocket and held it in his hand. That made the jailor laugh; the hand that used to hold gun, bent hillock now held flower ! He felt optimistic that such a ferocious youth would certainly return to path, the way of the world.

-Madam…. would feed…. me. Jambhira uttered so slowly that the words won't get dashed against the wind and be hurt.

Taken aback, the jailor asked,"Madam? Who is she?

As Jambhira remained silent, the jailor drew his attention to the women employees of the jail and said, "Who among them do you want to feed you?"

Jambhira nodded his head in negation and slowly said: "Madam, in charge of the police station."

Startled, the jailor looked at him, his eyes and marked as if the glow-sign of Shephali madam reflected. He was flabbergasted and at his wits' end. He felt the rules of the Criminal code got a topsy-turviness, as it were. It appeared, the emotion that Jambhira's eyes expressed, transformed the entire jail into a Kadamba tree. Anyone who heard this, turned fragrant like Kadamba flowers.

The jailor got back to reality and said sternly, "No, she won't come here. And why should she? How is she related with your taking food?"

Jambhira was wordless. But the language of his silence sounded Bishmilla Khan's sahanai and Hariprasad Chourasia's flute.

The jailor was determined not to put up with such insolence. But the news got wings. Shephali got drawn into the boundary of such metamorphosis that she had occasioned. She embraced it as a challenge. Crossing the police station, squares and staring eyes of hundreds of men, she reached the prison. Bypassing all rules and regulations, she took the plate of rice from the jailor and handed it over to Jambhira. She determined to complete the change she initiated.

Jambhira saw her in his front, his face calm and eyes mesmerized as though it experienced a stream of tenderness cascading!

- Take it and eat! With these grave words, Shephali handed over the plate to Jambhira which the latter held happily and started relishing the food with contentment. Beside herself with joy, she smiled and retraced her steps hastily. But she looked back all on a sudden, Jambhira was gulping down the food looking at her.

- Sir, didn't the Kadamba tree bear rose flower there? Kisan Sing said. Meghasan heard it meditatively.

Then Kisan Sing continued- The jailor reported everything from A to Z to the government. However, the incident was fabricated differently at different places. As Shephali madam's husband heard one such fabrication, he rushed to her. Seething in anger, he broke two to three of the twigs of the Kadamba tree and fumed, "O, you conspire to snatch my wife away from me!" Heaving a deep sigh, he burst out that the earth should be free of Kadamba tree.

The environment of the police station was in sixes and sevens just as the sky is disturbed with the rain lightning and thunder in rainyseason. Shephali madam was transferred within twenty-four hours and it was mandated that the order be carried out with immediate effect.

Hearing it Jambhira went deep into silence. Then he

repeated 'Madam, madam, madam, madam......'
Consequently he was admitted to a mental hospital.

As Kisan Sing stopped, Meghasan drew a deep breath.

For thousands of years the tree has been creating innumerable legends, histories in the midst of its enchanting circle. Meghasan saw through the window that the tree looked semi-darkened from the light post nearby. Folding hands he soliloquized -"Hello, Kadamba tree, how do you look upon me? Are you merciful?" Then he became strong and said, "No, a police station can't bow down to you. Now I take back my question."

Kisan Sing started, "Sir, the miracle of the Kadamba tree was not over. Akar Bhatt took charge of this police station after Shephali madam was transferred. He was your immediate predecessor, very capable. As he heard everything about the tree he turned pensive: the Kadamba tree and the police station maintain animus. As long as the tree is here, there is every possibility of recurring incidents like that of Shephali madam's. He wrote to the government that the police station needed two more rooms. And such expansion needed more space on which stood the Kadamba tree. Hence the tree be replaced or cut. He sent this proposal with map, graph and estimate.

At this point of narration, Kisan laughed loudly. It indicated to contain a mystery. Now Meghasan became an exact witness to Kisan's words, behaviour and gestures. He looked at him and perceived that whatever be Kisan's narration it had an unmistakable link with his uncontrollable laughter.

-Sir, then came a letter from the government that read, "It is strange you are planning how to do away with a Kadamba tree on the premises of your police station instead of planning to put down criminal activities in your jurisdiction." Akar Bhatt was dumbfounded. Thereafter he paid respect to the tree before he entered the police station. His staff followed him. His demeanour such as this was only outward. Inwardly he wondered that a tree could control a police station !

Families of the officers of the police station were very happy. A sort of fragrant enchantment captured them. Even the accused praised the tree. The rage that some other police stations used to fling was almost nil here.

The historic legend of Shephali Roy had already become a collective memory. Many addressed the police station, "O, that Kadamba police station !"

It was a rainy evening punctuated by occasional lightning and thunder. All lights were out except the light in front of the police station that functioned with battery. It was quite dark below the Kadamba tree. Someone was digging all around it with a spade. But the digging sound was drowned in rain and splashing of water. After some minutes he left the place cautiously. Five to seven minutes later, the same person came to the tree again with the spade, bucket, and mug. He scattered the earth around the tree, collected water with a mug and poured it into bucket. At times he paid homage to the tree and mumbled, "Please forgive me." Then he left the place with his articles.

By the time Kisan Sing finished his narration, Meghasan was excited. He wondered the tree was so powerful that a stubborn police officer like Akar Bhatt was discomfited!

- Sir, Akar sir experienced the condition, a defeated man suffers from as he envisages the winner always. The moment the Kadamba tree appeared before him, he was compelled to pay respect to it. So, how long could he have stayed here under such circumstances? He sought a transfer. You succeeded him. Kisan Sing said and remained silent.

Meghasan had reclined onward in the chair but now he reversed his position. Kisan Sing was in a hurry to return home.

Sir, this much I know about the Kadamba tree. I don't know if anybody has any other experience about it. Let me go now.

Meghasan said, "Many thanks. Please meet me whenever you come here."

Since the old Kisan Sing sat there for a long time he felt ache in his waist. He stood up with much difficulty. As he was about to stride onward, Meghasan requested him to sing that song again.

Kisan Sing warbled, " Kadamba malinam Krushnam gyayante naasti durgati" and left. He halted near the Kadamba tree for a while. A line of smile sparkled his lips.

After he heard the history of the Kadamba tree, Meghasan remained sceptical always. The tree looking through the window appeared to be a mysterious magician that could ensnare him anytime. How could the tree exert its supremacy over the police station even though it was none of the four pillars of a state such as legislature, executive, judiciary and the mass media ? Meghasan considered the tree his adversary and turned grave. Let the tree have its way and the police station its own. Let them not depend on each other, he wished.

At ten o' clock in the night two constables reached him with two fifteen year old adolescents bubbling with youthfulness. Both of them were students of class ten. The constables told that they caught them when they were trying to reach the roof of a person's house by climbing the mango tree that was behind the one- storey building.

Meghasan seated the boys on a bench and said, "Confess, why you tried to do this."

The two remained silent and stooped. Their faces appeared sullen and bloodless.

- See, you are school students. The more you delay; the worse will be your trouble. Media men roam around the police station. They will show your photos on television and you will earn bad names. So, confess soon, very soon, Meghasan warned them sternly.

Though the first boy was frightened, he supplicated, "Sir, please save us."

-Yes, we are here for that. Now you confess.

The boy told with much constraint, "Sir, Kalabati, a second year plus two student. She is older than us. She belongs to our street. Once we had passed comments on her. So...." The boy stopped there.

-Well, proceed. Said Meghasan.

As the boy kept mum, Meghasan warned, "Confess, otherwise you would repent throughout your life."

Now the second boy opened his mouth slowly and said, "Sir, we are not guilty because we had only held one's water pipe. Is it a crime?

-No, but it may be a plan to commit a crime. Is it ethical to climb someone's roof holding the water pipe at the back side of his house by night without his knowledge? Do you deserve any award for this?

The boy lowered his face and said, "Sir, whenever we came across her she would behave and expose herself in such feats that we got excited at night. Consequently we became weak. So we thought to reach a climax rather than being pestered every day.

-What sort of climax? Rape or murder? Or both? Meghasan asked investigatingly.

-No Sir. We would have begged apology with a request that she should not trouble us anymore.

Meghasan burst into a loud laughter. The constables too. He said," You write down on a piece of paper all that you said and put your signature. Since you are juvenile, you would be sent to reformatory. Now we will intimate your guardians over phone. They will come. Ok?"

The boys were afraid. Tears in eyes, they implored Meghasan to save them. The first boy said," Sir, please forgive us this time. Be not unkind to punish us for a flimsy fault."

Meghasan nodded his head that indicated negation. He tried to appear graver. He stroked his moustache twice.

The second boy mustered courage and said, "Sir, how can a person intending to beg apology be a guilty?

-Why should one beg apology unless one is assailed by a sense of guilt?

Just then the wind carried the fragrance of the Kadamba flower, which the two boys along with Meghasan and the two constables inhaled. All of them looked exuberant and sweet. The constables looked at Meghasan intently.

-Stand up, he said. The boys obeyed.

- "Don't commit such mistake again. Kalabati will not trouble you anymore. I shall deal with her." Be off Meghasan grunted.

Much startled, the boys ran away praising Meghasan. "Since the Kadamba tree emitted fragrance, Meghasan Sir cooled down soon," they expressed.

The constables uttered "Sir..Sir.." in the manner of showing signs of disapproval of the decision of Meghasan in the case.

-Do you think I should implicate the boys in the case

and ruin them? Go and find out who that Kalabati is. Warn her not to entice the boys any more. They have suffered a lot. Meghasan said.

Then he looked straight at the Kadamba tree and mumbled. "The tree has become an integral part of the police station. Let us recognize its existence."

Not only Meghasan's admission, but also everywhere it was known that the real in charge officer of Karkas police station was the Kadamba tree, all officials were its branches, leaves only.

Some wise men expounded, "What's new about it? The tree has controlled, guided and shaped mankind, its civilization and culture. What better is there than a Kadamba tree creating the history of Karkas police station? It's a world record."

It was wee hour that day. The street lights still burning, appeared like scarecrows standing alone under the cover of fog. As it dawned, a strange scene was seen at Karkas police station. The entire Kadamba tree was filled with flowers and a young man's body was hanging from one of its branches. The premises of the police station was filled with hullaballoos. The young man was no more. He was no other than the lunatic Jambhira. Somehow he had fled the mental ward and committed suicide in the dead of night.

The news spread like wildfire.

Hearing it, Shephali Roy, posted to the capital, drove herself in her car and reached the place. She became very much aggrieved as she saw such a catastrophe to the change she had initiated at Karkas police station. With a heavy heart she plucked a lot of Kadamba flowers and offered them to Jambhira. She sobbed uncontrollably and started pounding blow after blow on the Kadamba tree. The women officials of the police station took her care immediately.

Free from sentimentality, Shephali looked at the Kadamba tree, strengthened herself, and soliloquised, "Indeed, this incident is distressful. But it is the germination of a change. I have to go forward, more and more."

Meghasan sent Jambhira's dead body for post-mortem, sat down in his chamber and looked at the Kadamba tree. He contained his overflowing emotion and accumulated anger; drew out a sheet of paper and wrote: The Kadamba tree on the premises of the police station is arrested as it caused perpetual obstruction to dutiful police officers to discharge duties by creating in them undue mental pressure.

The Primeval Mother

Bunches of flowers stooped.They bore the existence of nature in an environment having no distnct separation of light and darkness. Jhumpa gazed intently at the swinging flowers on one side and the Robot-Jhumpa, her duplicate on the other. It was breastfeeding her son. And the child sucked gleefully. She felt no acute distinction between the flower and the Robot except in the sphere of knowledge.Is not man made thing under man? People had the wont of appointing ayas to bottlefeed their babies. Jhumpa tested her milk in a laboratory after she had known breastfeeding conducive to a child.Then she ordered a world famous robot company to make a replica of her and arranged a separate breast feeding means. She felt relieved as the Robot of her choice took her son's responsibility which she cosidered atrocious. Her husband, at times, embraced the Robot-Jhumpa as it resembled her incredibly. And as the Robot snatched its hands, it burst into immeasurable laughter.The contrivance could do everything, from feeding the child to making it fall asleep, fondling it in its lap when it cried, changing its panties when it urinated, etc.But at night Jhumpa made the child sleep at her side by swiching off the Robot and derived filial love. For fun, at times she would switch off the Robot-Jhumpa when it breast-fed and lo, the child cried inconsolably !

Then she would switch on and the child would be normal. So continued feeding the child. But later she marked the child getting confused by looking at similar appearances of the robot and herself as and when she approached it.The child would also turn surprised when it saw the two Jhumpas. It would look at one for a moment and the other then. Jhumpa felt shocked. Would the child develop two-personalities as it was being reared by two mothers, apparently similar? She apprehended. She also marked the child was somewhat reluctant to return to the Robot after she herself fondled her in her lap. She has also marked distinct expressions on the child's face. Did the child fell the difference between the mechanical touch of the Robot and the intimate emotional touch of her body ? But she was undone. She must discharge the responsibilities of managing director of a company. She was busy always with the internet for hours together. So was Mayur, her husband, busy in his company work. Stayed outside most of the time. She would see him on the internet too. Jhumpa felt it terribly. She heaved a deep sigh. Alas! the child would recognise its father from the internet and feel its mother from the robot-mother!

She compared her childhood with the childhood of her son. True, there was distance between an individual and an individual in her times but one was able to be emotional transcending such distance. But now machine was the means of relation between man and man. However, she used to take care of the child whenever she got leisure. She would engage the robot otherwise at that time.The child must be anxious for its mother as it is born of her DNA. She explained to Mayur. "We are born human beings; rearing the child is our topmost responsibility. Moonbeams, sunshine, fruits are more precious than the moon, the sun, and the tree. Alike, our child is more precious than us. We should devote more time to the child." Smiling, Mayur replied-" I know it pretty well,this is a plea -you desire me near you in the pretext of child rearing. But I do'nt know why you nurse such a passion .You have so many male friends and even a robot partner. Still, are you not satisfied? - Satisfaction? There would be no invention, were man be satisfied with machines and animality. Man would not have been hungry to be absorbed in flower garden, azure sky and shore for relief. The tragedy now is we have annihilated nature all around and have manufactured a commercial nature instead. And we have turned ourselves into tourists to get rid ot it. Hills, jungles, seas, deserts and ancient artistic objects have been sustenance of our life.

Mayur shut his eyes as Jhumpa completed.He was just listening.Silence reigned for a while.- "Do'nt use such dead language. Leave your job and take care of the child. Even you may take a divorce." Mayur expressed without an iota of excitement. Even water in a tank in a winter evening wo'nt be so cool. Jhumpa cast a glance at Mayur. She felt helpless. There was no difference among Mayur, theman, Mayur, the machine, Mayur, the tree-she thought. She switched off the robot, took the child in her lap and went to the cluster of flower plants. Mayur felt insulted by Jhumpa's such demeanour; he felt he was defeated, a persona non grata. Jhumpa's love for the child was more precious than his wealth and efficiency, as it were. And Jhumpa was exultant for this! This thought stung him so much that he rushed towards Jhumpa stormily. His physical movement shook the green leaves of the flower plants.

-Do you think I have no contribution towards the son? He flung a question.

Jhumpa looked at him and could read the emotion

darting in his eyes. She smiled heartily and said, "Do I deny?" She handed over the child to Mayur- "Take your son". As Mayur placed the child on his bosom, she burst into the giggles. It pierced Mayur's heart. He felt as if Jhumpa got a victory again, handing over the child to him. It was not good, now it was his turn to face a challenge. He fondled the child, kissed. Jhumpa's heart melted as she saw it; her face got enlivened. She chuckled heartily which expressed neither conquest nor defeat. Mayur's face also got brightened.He took the child to the robot nurse. As he switched it on, the Robot-Jhumpa took the child upstairs. He looked at it bewitched.

Jhumpa ran to him from the otherside and shook his hand violently. She was thoroughly upset. She asked. "Is this good ? Is it our son's mother?" Her words expressed her mental agony and annoyance. She felt envious of the Robot-Jhumpa. She thought, may be her husband had taken her a substitute wife far beyond a nurse. She fumed and fret.

Mayur tried to console her, "Why getting tense about it? See, you have made the robt-nurse-maid after your image.So that the child would experience mother and nursemaid simultaneously.Why find fault with me?"

Jhumpa kept mum; the device that she had adopted for the son's wellbeing has turned into a problem for her. Rather it would have been better were she not a mother. Such argument didn't satisfy her and a deep sigh shot from some unknown depth in her.

After some days. Jhumpa returned from abroad. She fumed in excessive anger and agony. Because Mayur had gone back on his promise. Putting the son in the Robot-Jhumpa's care he had been away for forty-eight hours.Though servants and menials were there. Jhumpa sat down without changing clothes. She informed Mayur over phone, she wo'nt take any food or even a glass of water till he returned home. Even she wo'nt change her clothes.

Mayur appeared jolly on the disc of the phone. As if he expressed : Look Jhumpa! I am so indispensable to you." Jhumpa got irritated, kept the phone in anger. Her nostrils got fulminated and she started swinging herself in the swing, "Strange, you left the son with the Robot-jhumpa for full forty-eight hours thinking it to be your wife and your child's mother!" She was in a whirlpool of thought, quite oblivious of the speed of the swing. As she heard a car screeching into a halt on the portico, she rose in no time and switched off the Robot-Jhumpa loitering on the veranda with the son. The robot fell silent. She snatched away the child from its lap and made it sleep on a sofa in the drawing room. She stood before the mirror with annoyance. As if she had turned into a lioness waiting to pounce on Mayur the moment he entered the room. Addressing her 'darling' repeatedly, Mayur entered the room. He was astounded when he saw the child on the sofa and Jhumpa in such a rare mood. Dumbfounded, he marked her face ablaze. Unable to meet her eyes, he lowered himself. Then raised his eyes and lowered again. He approached her slowly and said calmly, "See, your son, nay our son is safe and sound. Is'nt it?" Jhumpa remained silent as usual. Mayur tried to pacify her, "Look, it is necessary now to keep the child away from its parents gradually to enable it to be self dependant. Am I right?" Still Jhumpa stayed put. Deliberately Mayur sneezed time and again to avoid any possible explosion. But to no avail. Mayur felt exasperated and said in a slightly raised voice,"Please be normal if you swear to be silent. Don't look so terrible. I never compelled you to be mother."

- I too didn't compel you to be father! Jhumpa thundered that shook the entire environment as it were. The child asleep on the sofa broke into sobbing. Neither Jhumpa nor Mayur paid heed to it.They were hell-bent on denigrating each other.

- I don't want such an irresponsible person to be the child's father.

- I don't want a woman engaging a second wife in stead of a nursemaid as my wife.

The child was crying bitterly non-stop.

What's its final solution? Asked Jhumpa excitedly.

- That, too, is my question to you, Mayur retorted in a similar vein. He advanced towards Jhumpa as if he would slap her! Jhumpa too. Both confronted each other being least concerned about the child's cry that made the place pathetic more and more.The entire earth, water, air, animal kingdom- all eager to don the mantle of the mother, it appeared.

Suddenly the Robot-Jhumpa emitted a sound. It turned active, moved forward and took the child in her lap.Jhumpa couldn't believe her eyes, she had switched it off ! How could it become active as she had switched it off by the remote controller! She ran to the table, caught the remote controller to switch off the robot again. But the Robot-Jhumpa was going outside fondling the child in its lap. Mayur too felt such a strange occurrence.

- Mayur! See the robot is still active even though I have switched it off. Jhumpa expressed.The couple had no more irritation, retort. Mayur rushed and switched off the circuit of the robot and the main switch of the computer while Jhumpa was shouting 'nurse-maid' again and again.The domestic- helps rushed to the spot. But strangely the Robot-Jhumpa paced onward fondling the son at its breast.

■

Species

Seemadri pulled a mirror from a small shelf near his bed. Intently he looked at his face in it. His face bulged.

He soliloquized, "Yes. It's all right."

He kept the mirror on the cot, sat cross-legged, kept his palms straight on the bed and turned his head, chest and belly upside down. He deeply breathed and turned grave.

He spoke to himself- "I am a lion, leontiasis..........yes!" He wanted to roar like a lion.

Gradually he breathed normally and got rid of excitement. Baida, a patient, next to his bed was rearranging the bandage around his leg and asked- "Are medical students visiting you today?"

Seemadri replied with an emphatic "yes" exuding pride and continued, "Not only they but also some members of the World Health Institute. They will photograph me and make video recording. Would probably do something more. There is no other leontiasis like me. I am a lion." He expressed conceitedly. It seemed as if it's a blessing to be a leprosy patient having the face of a lion.

In fact, he felt himself to be a lion in this private charitable leprosy home and hospital. Medical students, researchers from different corners of the country and abroad visited him regularly. They used to talk to him and note down the genesis of leprosy on his body, the pains he suffered from it and acquaint themselves with the reality of how a leontiasis looked. That's why, Seemadri thought himself as a special and rare species.

Everyone in this hospital - doctors, nurses, attendants and even the district and state level officials also paid special attention to his case and treatment. So that he won't feel that he was neglected. Such significant care towards him was catalytic to garner a proud feeling that he was a lion. And the hospital also became famous in the country and beyond for him too. Thus the hospital enjoyed the advantage of receiving financial assistance from different levels. The hospital, its patients, doctors and officials went on reaping benefits. Thus we may attribute Seemadri to be the light of the institution.

Some medical students arrived. They stood around Seemadri's bed in a semicircular shape. Seemadri stretched his legs, rested his hands on the two sides of the bed, and started swaying his chest. Prof. Chaturbedi explained to the students: Listen, this patient with a lion's face is not only second in the state but also in the country. The other one is Ramanathan now at Karimal hospital.

: Here you see, half of his forehead has become hairless. Alopecia of both eyebrows. Eyelashes are hanging and hairs fallen. See, both eyes lagophthalmos, unable to close. Left eye is damaged. He can see only with his right eye.

: See also, the bridge of his nose has shrunk beneath and nostrils have become small.

: See, his moustache is discontinuous and beard is of the same feature. His face is awkward and ugly, suffering from facial palsy; his cheeks on both sides are hung.

: Look at his ears, swollen, earlobes hanging. His entire

visage is hypo- pigmented. Well, you all should see intently. See, how his face is lion-faced."

The students agreed while one of them said, "Sir, we feel happy that we could visit a leprosy patient having leontiasis face." This made Seemadri extremely irritated. "I suffer from the most tormenting state of leprosy and you feel happy!" He thought. His eyes turned more violent and virulent. Yet he kept mum. Thought, yes, medical students need to cherish interest to know about new diseases and visit such patients. That's what they did. Two students photographed him in different poses and did video recording too.

A student told another: See, all the fingers and toes of both sides are mutilated. Hands and legs have become stumps due to lack of proper care and treatment.

Her friend replied, "The most important matter about this disease is the patient's hatred of his affected limbs. Since such limbs lose the power of sensation, gradually he develops a sense of apathy towards it. That invites all trouble."

In the meantime an old woman approached Seemadri's bed and stood silently. Prof. Chaturbedi introduced her to his students that she was Savitri, Seemadri's wife. Further he said, "In fact, she is Savitri who has snatched her husband from his grudge against life to a life to be loved just as the mythical Savitri had rescued her husband from the god of Death. In fact, she has turned him from a pessimist to an optimist."

Savitri paid obeisance in folded hands to all of them who also complimented her. Seemadri felt immeasurably proud to hear his wife's admiration. He started shaking.

The medical students noting down something took leave of Seemadri. Seemadri had swelled the storehouse of their knowledge.

The Superintendent of the hospital felt relieved and went to his chamber. He cautioned his colleagues to make the final preparation in connection with the afternoon visit of a team of the World Health Institute. They must shoulder their responsibilities and pay special attention to Seemadri, he reiterated. All including Seemadri knew it well that this group of medical students visited the hospital before the visit of the WHI team to activate the atmosphere, patients, and staff about such visit. Seemadri prepared himself in his thought- "Yes, I am lion faced......I am a lion. O, yes!" His entire body trembled. As his wife approached him, he became steady. He looked at the flower plants all around the hospital. Flowers dancing in the breeze like waves excited him. As a result, a sweet sensation throbbed him.

"I saw such flowers in my childhood
In my youth too;
Again when I became adult
Now I see them in my old age
But the same flower".
Then he consoled himself.

Three years after his marriage. On an afternoon he was sitting on a cot, worries writ large on his face. He called his wife near him and said: Savitri! Please kiss my right hand.

Savitri was taken aback and did as bidden again by her husband. Then drops of tear trickled down his eyes. Savitri anxiously asked, 'Oh, why did you cry?"

Seemadri left home instantly.

Yes, he went far, far away from his native village. He built a nettled cabin in the midst of thorny bush at a distant town. By that time he had developed facial palsy, claw fingers and drop foot. And bandaged his feet for plantar ulcers. He grew his moustache and beard to hide his identity.

That day. Picketing was going on due to spread of the freedom struggle. The police were at the heel of the agitators. Suddenly a freedom fighter rushed into his hut and asked him, "Please tell me where to hide myself."

Seemadri didn't reply and came outside. He stood exposing his disfigured hands, feet and face. The policeman stood there stupefied. Didn't enter his hut. He looked down upon Seemadri's physical diformity and uttered, 'Damn, it' and went away.

The freedom fighter came out of the hut and said, 'Well, you saved me from being arrested. Many, many thanks." Seemadri smiled, showed deformed limbs and said, 'Yes, you know everything .....' The former chuckled and departed. Seemadri could very well mark the note of indignation in the depth of his chuckle and cried. Also he whimpered bitterly. As if the entire humanity was against him and he was fighting his struggle for existence. All alone.

At times he would remember how Sabitri kissed his hand when he left home and looked intently at the spot of kissing, then slowly touched it and kissed it lovingly. And shed tear. As his limbs became insensitive he failed to feel the warmth of his tears and touch but his palpitation grew.

Though an atheist, he went to visit the car festival at Puri. Time and again he would ask himself. "Why and what for he is living pocketing so much hatred, so much contempt and so much indifference?" He failed to understand why he did not commit suicide. Ah, what a life it was, that had the capability to stand so much misery and adversity! He wondered. In fact, one can't measure the might of life force if one doesn't fall into terrible font of adversity. He would spend more on toddy, ganja, than on foods whatever he earned as alms. He also kept sexual relationship with four women suffering from leprosy. In fact these women left home and stayed like him in wretched huts. Yet Sabitri's kiss was unique. How? What for?

He desired to go to Puri's car festival only to earn money. Like previous times he grew his beard and moustache, so that nobody could recognize him.

He slept on a bed of thorns; threw burning faggots upward and held it in his bare hand, a trick to attract passersby towards him. The burning faggot hit his hand which got burnt. So also blood oozed from his back as the thorn of bed on which he slept pierced it. Yet he succeeded; earned much money from passersby. He concluded that the visible deformities of his limbs born of the disease were a means to eke out a living. He continued with it in places of fairs, festivals and earned too.

The scorching heat of the sun was waning at Puri. Seemadri was busy throwing a faggot upward, a feat which the onlookers nearby enjoyed. One of them intently looked at him. Then she screamed, "Alas! You, you!"

Sabitri's shout surprised her father and brother. She pointed at Seemadri, "You see, that man is he….." She burst into tears.

-What do you say? Is he Seemadri? Her father asked. "Yes", she said. The whole atmosphere turned pathetic. Her father and brother did not want that she should accept such a crippled leprosy patient as her husband again or identify as her husband. She should not also wallow in emotional misery for a man already wasted.

-Well, you simply behave as if you don't know him. You may go on crying for years together for him; pray to God for him, but don't reveal your identity to him, said her father.

But Sabitri remained adamant. She stuck to her promise -"Whether or not, you, my father and brother, extend your help, I shall rescue my husband from the claws of death," she said.

On being asked, Seemadri denied that he was Seemadri, though he experienced a surge of emotion in his heart of hearts. He suffered deeply and would suffer lifelong, yet why he should be a burden on Sabitri! Let her not suffer for his sake. Thinking so, he wanted to give a false identity. But Savitri's queries unravelled the truth. Sabitri, with the assistance of her father and brother got him admitted to this hospital.

Flowers danced, danced
In his childhood
In his youth
Now too
Though he was old.

Seemadri turned his eyes. He determined to strengthen himself mentally to meet the officials of the World Health Institution coming just now. Only to see him. He would be photographed. They would also make a video-recording. "He is having a leontiasis face amongst the deformed leprosy patients in the world now, he is a lion!" Seemadri trembled in excitement.

Sabitri stared at him and said, "Why getting excited so much ? You have heart problem, head reeling, Don't be so anxious!"

Seemadri fell silent, turned a bit normal. Adequate arrangements had been made to welcome the WHI officials. The hospital staffs were quite agog and agile. Designs and decorations had been completed. All patients appeard encouraged.

Suddenly superintendent of the hospital put an end to all such promptness and announced that the officials would not come. They cancelled their programme of visit.

Instead they went to Karimal hospital. They would visit Ramananthan - the patient having a leontiasis face and make a documentary on him.

Finishing this, the Superintendent heaved a deep breath. As Seemadri heard this, he became excited. Gnashed his teeth. He shouted, "Rubbish! Is Ramanathan bigger lion-faced than I? Hum!"

He roared like a lion and fell on the bed all on a sudden.

■

A Cartography

The sun was about to set. Clad in a clean dhoti Bhika Saanta (grandpa) was sauntering, his dhoti tucked around his waist and stretched up to knees. A white towel he had tied around neck. He held a bamboo staff in left hand and a big basket in right hand. The basket was full of rice, some blades of grass, sweetened flat rice, a sickle, etc. He was eighty yet robust altogether. Till now his chest functioned well. Unlike other aged persons he never cursed his fate and God.

Slowly he passed along the road at the village end. He had already crossed the islet in the river bed, cluster of palm trees. Now he moved to left at Barunapada. He sank totally as he approached the paddy field having jack fruit trees on the border. He kept the basket at the corner of the paddy field. He did not cut ten paddy plants at the corner of the plot for the annual ritual to be performed at the corn field after harvest. He divided those plants by two and intertwined five paddy plants with the other five. And worshipped it ritually by keeping blades of grass, rice, some betel nuts on the knot and prayed. He offered a portion of the sweetened flat rice kept in sal leaves and scattered the rest all around the paddy field.

It was twilight, almost dusky. Silence reigned everywhere. Bhika Saanta prostrated before the knot and pushed his head between the two bundles of paddy plants. Below him were the earth and above the knot of those bundles. Bhika cut the roots of those paddy plants. He paid obeisance to the field, hung the two bundles on his neck, held his staff and the basket that contained articles of worship, and returned home along craggy boundary ridges of paddy fields.

Members of his family burst into laughter as they saw him in such appearance. Shayari, his granddaughter asked him to wait a bit and made him stand at the threshold. She then photographed him and thanked. She was pursuing a Smile Designer course in Mumbai. How much and how long a person need to smile to look beautiful, both covertly and overtly and which type of smile is required to match one's expression mainly constituted her syllabus of study. She herself fixed an extra tooth at the right side gum to look attractive. She was researching on types of laughter of different animals, grass, trees and human, the science of smile.

In fact, man has turned disgusted with hypocritical laughter exuded every moment. That has also resulted in some people's strange critical health disorder and ailment. So Shayari has taken up such a study to delve deep into the matter. But Bhika Saanta did not know the ABC of her research. Nor did he care it. His sole desire was to see her wedding. Eager to have a grandson-in-law. After seeing his great grandson or daughter he would leave the earth peacefully and get salvation; he believed in such traditional faith.

Shayari enquired him of the ritual of worship he performed at the paddy field. Bhika Saanta presented a comprehensive explanation. He said, "It was to show respect to earth, corn field and harvest. Respect connotes victory."

The entire family was proud of Bhika Saanta. They were also vigilant about him. He was the oldest person in the village and though above eighty, he very rarely suffered. He was a moving history, indeed! Not only he had knowledge of the rituals for each festival but he did it. At times his grandsons and grand daughters encouraged him for this. They compared his times with theirs. They would feel the past through him. He was not merely their grandpa but was also a living monument, archeology. They loved, cared and protected him as well. Unlike other grandchildren they would never criticise him as an old-timer. But they did quite opposite! For them their grandsire was a moving lexicon, a rare treasure. They were ready to jot down whatever he told about the rituals of festivals. They said, "We would write treatises and make films using these. We are interested to learn about the shapes and contours of humans before fifty thousand years ago; it must also be a matter of eager inquisition to know about the living styles, of grandpa and his ancestors."

Bhika Saanta cleaned his hands and legs with tube-well water. Then he changed the dhoti he had put on, covered his body with a piece of cloth printed with the sacred names of Hare Krishna, Hare Rama and hang a rosary of holy basil around his neck.

Shayari asked, "Grandpa! What use if one puts on this sort of cloth piece and beads?"

-Well, one's psyche gets spiritually exalted if one wraps one self with such a peice of cloth. We repeat names of the Lord just as you enjoy yourselves putting on banians with pictures of Tendulkar, Michel Jackson on these. And about the beads- it emits a supernal scent just as you smear powder on your body for fragrance, said he.

Shayari took breath, thought for a while and said,

"Grandpa! You are too much traditional, an old timer."

-If the history of the piece of cloth I have worn is about five thousand years and that of yours is about five thousand and fifty years, then tell me which is older?

Shayari got puzzled, remained speechless. Now she realized the truth of what Grandpa said.

Bhika Saanta entered his room of worship sporting a smile and started chanting God's name. Then he returned and sat on the dining chair. Shayari was watching a cricket match on TV. Her mother kept a plate of semolina halva and a glass of water before Bhika. The old man removed the spoon and took the food in his hand. Seeing it Shayari burst into laughter. If her grandfather would live for about forty more years, the children could know about the social evolution of his times, she brooded.

Ramani, Bhika's wife performed her evening worship and sat beside the hearth. She pushed a cake of cow-dung and some pieces of fuel wood into the hearth and lit them with a tin lamp. As the fire caught the fuel Ramani folded her hands and paid respect to the fire and hearth. The smoke vanished and the fuel started burning. Shouting her name at the back door, her neighbour Khira's mother asked her if she had lit her hearth. Without waiting for Ramani's answer she came in, took a bundle of fire and left in no time.

-Hello, why didn't you stay for a while? Ramani entreated.

-No, it's already your brother's teatime. Slight delay would irritate him.

No sooner had she left, than Parima another neighbour appeared with a bundle of hay and set it on fire inside the hearth, blew it to burn and left murmuring a casting look at Ramani : One generation goes high, while another goes down, let the water flow ; a hearsay. Ramani withdrew herself and gave her way.

The two families were not on speaking terms as they had fallen out for a tree for the last five days. Yet Parima never felt uneasy to lit her bundle of hay everyday with the fire in Ramani's hearth. This is the alchemy of soulful affinity. Who can evade it? Soul has no enemy. One feels utterly fallen if and when such relationship becomes loose. In fact, if somebody lights her hearth, it's shared by neighbours betokening the effulgence of intimacy.

Parima's daughters in law visited her next afternoon when her husband was not at home. Did her daughter encounter any adversity ! She apprehended as they came at an odd time. She was known as a quarrelsome lady. Pari's father Sudura was a salesman in a cloth store. Parima felt nervous, how to entreat them ! She had nothing at her home. She felt terribly upset even when she handed over them jugs of water to wash their feet and a towel to wipe water. By that time her neighbours were already present at her home of their own accord. They greeted the guests and placed fish curry, brinjal fry, green leaf fry, curd, papad, etc. in Parima's kitchen for their hospitality. Parima's relatives relished everything with utmost satiety. They were not surprised because they knew how one's guests there were indeed guests of all. The neighbours remained related even in the teeth of their bickering, suits filed in courts, etc. Lo, Ramani too treated them with the tasty curry of big gudgeon fish.

This was how the villagers were tied to one another. And its memory brightened Bhika's visage and excited him as well. He heaved a deep sigh as he reminisced the life fifty years back. Three days back Buddha, his related brother visited his home. Bhika's son Jara asked him if he came with a purpose.

-No, no. Just I came; said Buddha.

- Well, I have a lot of work to do, replied Jara. Buddha loitered for a while and turned to leave. Bhika saw all this and felt embarrassed. He requested him to stay for some time so that they would converse. But Buddha left at once. Bhika could fathom man's angst of existential hiatus. One even didn't speak to another if one had no necessity! Nor one addressed the other cordially! Moreover, one didn't offer a cup of tea to the other if one had no purpose to be served! Oh ! Time had become man's treasure, his property, his capital. One could spend it as one wished. Relationship was measured commercially!

Such awesome experience froze him terribly. He gasped- O, the time, O the manners! Yesterday five or six persons came to his neighbour by a car. But nobody did know who they were and what their whereabouts were. What to speak of sending eatables in hospitality for them! Khira's grandson abducted a girl from Madras and kept her in his house. It came to light when police came for investigation.

Bhika Saanta wondered- What transformation! Who transformed everything? A volley of questions confounded him lock, stock and barrel. Was he not changed? Had not hair on his head turned white? Why was the mango luscious in his childhood, tasteless now? He finished taking food served by his daughter-in-law and felt fatigued. He cast a glance at Sayari who looked at her laptop and wrote down something. Bhika Saanta approached her and saw pictures of different types of laughter on the lap-top.

-Grandpa! The types of laughter you see here are natural. Just see now- the calf ran to the cow that smiled gleefully. Look at its eyes, mark its laughter! Now look at the monkey also. It has held a cucumber in its hands. It laughs. Look how its teeth emit a smile of delight ! she said.

Bhika Saanta looked at the monkey intently. And then at Sayari. He felt content that his granddaughter was engaged in a new venture. He asked her, "Well, have you any other type of laughter to show me?"

Sayari ran her fingers on the laptop that flashed green grass drenched with dew drops. She enlarged the picture and said, "Grandpa! See how bright and cheerful the blade of grass is!

As the old man saw it, he said, 'When would you make me laugh?'

- "How silly! You laugh always, therefore your age also laughs." Sayari said.

-O, no! You know it very well what I ask for?

-Truly speaking, Grandpa! I chose three young men but rejected them. Because one was impotent while the other had blind filial love and the third was lascivious. Sayari jolted.

-How could you know all this? Bhika asked her surprisingly.

-From my experience of relationship with them for months together. She replied coolly without compunction.

Bhika Saanta was at his wits' end, his face turned pale. Sayari marked it and said, "Well, Grandpa! Why are you flabbergasted? Had you no girl friend?"

Bhika smiled and thought, now he would unravel what he could not do when his wife Ramani alive. He was fourteen when he saw Baishnab's daughter Ketaki on the road. As she passed by him, he turned and looked at her. Ketaki, a girl of nine only then. But she had covered her entire body with a piece of sari.

That evening his father tied him to a pillar and beat him black and blue. His body turned red with bruises galore. He suffered from fever for three days. For thirteen days, the ache on his body remained. He couldn't see anyone face to face for three months. Times were so then when it was as arduous nay impossible to talk to girls as was blossoming a lily in the ocean.

Sayari cackled as she heard her grandpa. She thought he would faint if she narrated the way she behaved with her boyfriend to gauge his sexiness. But she didn't say anything and remained silent smilingly. The night was getting late. Bhika Saanta wanted some clarification from her. He asked, "Then whom would you marry?"

-A monkey. It would be an inter- animal marriage. No problem. We have already accustomed to the tradition of marrying a tree (Sahada Sundari)-she expressed.

-You may marry whom you desire. But I want a grandson soon. Bhika said angrily and retired to his room.

Suman, the tiger was wandering in the dense forest where a river flowed. The forest had electric light posts at places. Hills and the woods stretched for miles. A tank in between. The zoo was the habitat of animals and birds, elephants, crocodiles, lions, other animals and different kinds of birds. It used to attract innumerable tourists who liked boating in the lake. Suman loitered there. It was being taken care of by attendants. Doctors used to examine its health day and night. It was given meat twice a day. It was wandering and yawning. Sometimes it enjoyed sex with the tigress Raila and slept then. Hale and hearty, it would run from this side to that side of the strong iron fence where it halted. So it was running by its side. It was very eager to cross the fence. Everybody wants to cross limit.

Suman got tired. It sat beside the fence and fell asleep gradually. It yawned when it got up. It felt hungry and returned to its den where it would swallow meat, feel contented and smile. A signboard hanging on its den read:

"National Animal". If Suman understood it, it would jump in joy, puffed with pride as the national animal, thousand times a day.

Sayari showed her grandpa these moods of Suman flashed on her laptop. Bhika remarked immediately: Look, how it is so anxious to go beyond the iron fence!

-Look grandpa, how the animal lives with ease and comfort. Has it got a body for this? She said and looked at him intently but didn't mark any reaction on his face. She continued, "The tiger is fed to live. It has been preserved just as mango pickle is preserved. Understand? If it lives this way, it would be a different animal, not tiger in later years. It won't have this sort of face or moustache or claw", she said.

Bhika Saanta withdrew from the place instantly. May be he thought something about this. He entered his room silently. Sayari was startled. She followed him. It was not that late night. Yet her grandpa lay in bed. She massaged his legs and asked if he suffered from any disease. She reminded him that he had given her words to narrate the story of the Koili (Cuckoo) festival.

- "It's no more in vogue. Why are you interested in it ? Do you want to observe it? Your study is about laughter and you want to make all smile. So, why bother about that festival?" He said.

- Grandpa! Laughter is the matrix of all. It is the genuine resource of civilization. Don't we derive it observing festivals? She said.

- Of course! While saying so, the scenes danced before Bhika: "The tiger Suman would swallow meat. Doctors would attend upon it when it suffered. Employees would be alert for its care. It would run in the forest and halt beside the iron fence. Then it would sleep there, get up and yawn.

Its eyes would glisten in sunrays. It would retreat a bit and see pieces of meat. It would laugh ...."

Suddenly Bhika Saanta's face became sullen. He could not narrate the story of the 'Koili (Cuckoo) Festival' to Sayari. The more he got care and affection in the family, the less became his laughter

He waited avidly to listen to the cooing of the cuckoo. And then only he would draw Sayari's attention to this.

BLACK EAGLE BOOKS

www.blackeaglebooks.org
info@blackeaglebooks.org

Black Eagle Books, an independent publisher, was founded as
a nonprofit organization in April, 2019. It is our mission to
connect and engage the Indian diaspora and the world at large
with the best of works of world literature published on a
collaborative platform, with special emphasis on
foregrounding Contemporary Classics and New Writing.